AND HE HEALED THEM ALL

A Day in the Life of the Teacher from Nazareth

A Novel

Jeffrey McClain Jones

And He Healed Them All

Copyright © 2014 by Jeffrey McClain Jones

All rights reserved. No part of this book may be reproduced in any form by any electronic or mechanical means including photocopying, recording, or information storage and retrieval without permission in writing from the author.

2nd Edition

John 14:12 Publications

www.john1412.com

Cover

by

Gabriel W. Jones

Photographic images courtesy of Getty Images.

To John Lehman, Sr. and Joanna, and the people of Reba Place Church from 1986 to 1999.

Chapter One
Only a Dream

I straightened my shirt collar for the fourth time, tried to slow my breathing, and wished I had somewhere to leave my coat. This is no time of year to make a good impression, I thought, looking down at my salt-and-snow-blotched shoes. I looked at the solid oak door in front of me, as if it could offer me some assurance that the occupant within that office would be glad to see me. But, then, I didn't even know if she was in there.

Previous conversations with Dr. Jillian Moore began to rerun in my mind's projector again. I fast-forwarded from one scenario to the next, imagining my smooth and sophisticated responses. It occurred to me that my persona in these little trailers to the movie that I wanted to be my life bore an embarrassing similarity to James Bond. I shook my head at that revelation. My internal disgrace killed my courage. I wasn't ready for this kind of emotional stretch. I stepped back from the door.

It opened.

The timing was such that it almost appeared that the door triggered on my step away from it, like an automatic door with a confused motion sensor. But I was the one looking confused now.

"James, is it?" A tall brunette in a gray wool skirt and dark gray cardigan greeted me.

I stared into her deep blue eyes, trying to remember the answer to her question.

"Ah, yeah. James. Walter's . . . friend." I hesitated over that last word, but it suited the situation better than the truth, which was much more complicated.

"Yes, of course. I remember who you are. It's just your name I wanted help with." She probably sensed my nerves.

Her comment about remembering me almost switched me over to my second agenda item, but I had this planned and stuck to my prepared comments, like a politician trying to defend his campaign.

"Well, I wanted to talk to you about Walter, if you have a minute." I glanced inside her office to see that she wasn't with someone already.

"I have a couple of minutes before my next appointment, come on in," she said.

As I walked into her colorfully and neatly decorated office, something occurred to me. "Were you headed somewhere? You opened the door before I knocked."

She smiled warmly. "No, I just thought I heard someone at the door. Sometimes a resident will come to my door and forget what they wanted. I've found a few people standing just where you were, talking to themselves."

Not having the excuse of senility, all I could do was smile at the coincidence and hope she couldn't read my mind as well as hear through doors. Swinging back to the reasons for my visit, I stepped over to a tan cloth-covered chair in front of her desk. She relaxed into her tall desk chair and waited for me to begin.

"I wanted to ask you about psychiatric medication for Walter. His doctor had said something about anti-depressants. What do you think? He seems so deflated these days."

Her pursed lips and narrowed eyes spoke sympathy for Walter and for my concern. "Yes, I'm aware of his mental state, especially after the doctor told him there was no hope of recovering from the stroke. It's completely understandable."

I could tell she was an ally in my cause. "Isn't there some measure of recovery he could be working toward? Wouldn't that help his mood?"

She nodded. "Actual recovery would be ideal, but even a hope of some improvement would help a lot. It's just his age that his doctor has in mind. At eighty-seven Walter is pretty weak and frail. I think that influenced his doctor's decision."

I knew he wasn't in great physical shape before the stroke, being a bookish person during his later years. Since his wife's death, he had given up hiking and canoeing, for which they had been known around campus when he was a professor.

"How do you know Walter?" she said.

"He was my favorite professor from college. In his Sociology of Religion class I first started questioning my conservative upbringing. He became my unofficial mentor and a good friend back then."

Jillian glanced at the clock, shortening my answer. "I'm sorry, but I do have to go and see someone about a fight." She laughed.

"Really?" I said, as I stood with her.

She grinned broadly and nodded, but then turned more serious. "I will give some thought to either pushing for physical therapy or maybe prescribing anti-depressants." She picked up a file from her desk. "I would prefer the former, of course, but insurance may favor the latter."

I surrendered a sigh at the mention of insurance and followed her out of the office. "I understand, and I appreciate your help. I guess I knew you'd have similar concerns."

"Of course," she said.

Then my blood pressure jumped as I calculated whether this would be an appropriate time for me to introduce my second reason for visiting her office. It seemed a stretch. We walked toward the front entrance.

"You said you had to deal with a fight?"

She gave me a quick glance. "Yes, they may be less energetic than they used to be, but we have an altercation to deal with every once in a while."

We stopped by the oversized wooden front doors, each glancing at the weather through the tall windows on either side.

"Thanks again for your help, Dr. Moore," I said, offering my hand.

"Please, call me Jillian. Otherwise, I'll have to call you Doctor . . ."

"Wolfer," I said and smiled.

"Dr. Wolfer."

This little exchange was just awkward enough for me to feel room to make that stretch. I grinned. "Well, if you promise not to call me Dr. Wolfer, maybe we could get together some time outside of this place." I scrapped my prepared speech in favor of attempted spontaneity.

She smiled, no hesitation, no awkward tightening around her mouth, just a smile. That encouragement launched a thousand hopes and left me a bit delirious.

"Sure, that would be nice," she said. "When did you have in mind?"

As soon as I was able to focus, we compared schedules briefly and settled on Friday, the next night, after work. I'd pick her up at her office. That would bring me back to see Walter again, a valuable side benefit, given my concern about his mental health.

**

That Friday night, ice-crusted snow crunched under my tires as I pulled into the parking lot of the Presbyterian retirement home for the second time that week. My new four-wheel drive car, unfazed by the elements, offered a fleeting sense of security on the dicey roads. I savored that comfort, even something as superficial as the tactile tug and unmistakable new-car smell.

If only I had some sense of security about Walter. Losing his hold on life, his weakened old hands were no longer able to grip firmly the world around him, though his mind remained sharp. Perhaps the pain of watching him struggle with a failing body, and knowing he could see it too, heightened my apprehension. He hid most of his feelings, but when he met his limits in opening a pill bottle, or needing something from the other side of the room, his eyes grew fierce and his lips pinched. I sometimes wondered if those wheelchair-bound elders who stared blankly into space weren't to be envied in their oblivion.

As I watched the demise of the one man who meant the most to me in the world, impending loss intruded upon the last days I would spend with him.

I swung through the door of the gray brick building, with its new blue carpet catching the late sunlight through wide lobby windows. The odor of disinfectant mingled with the new-carpet smell fused into a sense of foreboding for me. I walked past the empty reception desk toward the wing where Walter lived. There I knew I would find the nurses' station occupied. I smiled and said, "Hi," when the managing nurse straightened in her chair and flashed me a smile. "Good evening, Dr. Wolfer."

I kept walking, not slowing down to talk. My funk about Walter drove me to his room, where I hoped for some sign of life.

I never called him Walter when I was a student, of course. He was near retirement age then, and I, a straight-laced Midwestern kid with a strict Republican upbringing, spoke to him and of him with respect. But now I too was a professor at that same private Protestant college, and he insisted that I call him by his first name, as if my habit of addressing him more formally threatened to age him even faster than the calendar and gravity.

I stopped before his door, which hung open several inches. I peered in. He seemed to be asleep. A round, middle-aged nurse named Millie quietly removed a tray from next to his bed. Her big doll-like eyes glanced at me as she headed for the door.

Millie squeezed past me, leaned close, and whispered, "He's actually just waking up. He started opening his eyes when I got to him. But he pretended to still be asleep when he realized that it wasn't you."

I smiled and breathed a small laugh. "Maybe I should let him know that he can't fool you."

"Oh, he knows," she said.

I entered the room and rounded the bed to the window side. Walter's face was turned that way. Untidy gray loops of hair adorned his pale, bald pate. Once a robust man of a hundred eighty pounds and ruddy faced, he now seemed a faded, wrinkled copy of that hearty old friend.

Indeed he did open his eyes and smile when I stood by his bed. The significance of the smile, however, went beyond simply being glad to see me. He appeared more content in that small gesture than I had seen him in a long time.

"She's gone; you can 'wake up' now," I said, glancing at the exit through which Millie had disappeared.

He chuckled and slowly raised his left hand to wipe at his eyes. His stroke had rendered his right hand generally useless.

"After they poke and probe you enough times, you start to look for a place to hide when they come in. Sleep is my only refuge."

"Or faking sleep, if necessary." I crossed my arms over my chest.

"Yes." He nodded, waking up for real now. "But, you know, I had a dream last night that I didn't want to wake up from. It was so real, so vividly clear. I was really disappointed to find myself back here." He reached for his silver-rimmed glasses on the nightstand to his left.

The way Walter carefully maneuvered his glasses with one hand, reminded me of my father. I had lately been thinking about when I'd lost my father; about the cold, gray March day not long after his seventieth birthday, when I stood with my mother and sisters by the graveside. I was wrestling with the realization that I feared Walter's death more than I had my father's.

Even as I returned to this gloomy self-absorption, Walter—who was still very much alive—kept talking about his dream. But the bit that I heard hatched a new fear. Was he beginning to lose his mind?

"At first I thought I was just sort of flying over the hills and plains of eastern Iowa where I grew up, but then I saw rockier hills, more like giant piles of stones than mountains, and I knew I was somewhere else."

"Wait," I said, interrupting. "You're just talking about a dream you had last night?"

Walter rolled his eyes toward me and tipped his head. "Yes, a dream. But a dream like no other dream I've ever had." He peered at me over his glasses, his brow lowered in a barely patient pose.

He resumed his account. "Over those rocky hills swarmed people dressed in flowing robes of many colors and textures. It seemed like a part of Morocco or maybe Egypt. But they were all dressed in these ancient costumes; no T-shirts or baseball caps to break up the picture. It seemed to me then that I was viewing a scene from some day in long past history." He paused to take a breath. He stared over my shoulder, yet I got the impression that he wasn't looking through the window but replaying the dream in his head.

"These people all converged on a bundle of rocks at the top of a hill next to a dark blue body of water—a lake, I think. They seemed to be hurrying, like they were trying to be the first in line for something."

I sparred with how a dream could be so compelling as this one seemed to be for Walter. I pushed back at the thought that he was losing his grip on this world. I had heard of people having vivid dreams just before they died. This unusual subconscious foray from Walter seemed like one more sign that his life was near the end.

"It was like I was zooming over these people, flying over like a hawk. They were gathering from all directions, converging on this one hill, different kinds of people, people in groups, in families, and others traveling by themselves."

"Have you ever had a dream like this before? I mean, one so strangely vivid and so memorable?"

"Well, it's not any stranger than dreaming I'm in the bathroom at the president's house—president of the college, that is—and I can't get out, only to I realize I don't want to get out, because I'm not wearing any clothes." Walter chuckled. "Now that's a strange and memorable dream."

I laughed. "Well, at least you can identify the place, and you appear in that dream as yourself. This new dream seems sort of out of the blue. Did you see any movies like this recently, read any books with similar images?"

And He Healed Them All

He looked toward the corner of the room again in a moment of exploration. "No, that's not it. But it does seem out of the blue, doesn't it? That's what made it so different from the usual working through of psychological issues in my subconscious mind." He paused and nodded. "Oh, I still remember my basic psychology. I know where dreams usually come from. But I'm inclined to think that this is something different."

Walter could easily convince me of most things.

The last time I fought with him was when he advised me not to marry Debra, my now ex-wife. He thought we were mismatched. "Like an embarrassing pair of socks," he'd said. "She won't be there for you when it really counts, and you can't be supportive of her either, because she has no idea what she wants." That was a big fight.

I won the battle.

He won the war.

He never did say, "I told you so," not at any of the hundred points where his analysis proved true.

"Anyway," he said, "these people are running and walking, and carrying others on stretchers, or pulling them in little wooden carts. They're swarming toward this one spot. Then it was like I zoomed in to the scene at the top of that hill, where a small group of men stood. None of them seem particularly well dressed, compared with the crowd, but they seemed in command of the situation, as if they knew what was happening. Off to the side, next to the largest rocks on top of that hill, one man knelt, resting his chin in his hands. He didn't seem upset, just sort of getting away from the people. Maybe he was praying."

Walter sounded more like a witness recounting a real event than someone trying to catch hold of the mental mirage that describes most dreams.

He continued. "When that man stood up, I realized that the place he was standing was protected on three sides, with a wall of rocks the size of school buses behind him. This group of men in front of him formed a sort of barrier, like bodyguards. Just like with some kind of rock star, the people who had rushed to the top of the hill were reaching out their hands to this man. They called out to him, crying for him to help, begging for his attention.

"Then, in spite of this press, what appeared to be a woman with her son were let through the ring into the space where that man stood. The woman was tall and thin, with long dark hair under a light gray head covering, and the boy was about twelve or thirteen, not quite as tall as his mother. The man smiled at them, and the boy ran to hug him. At first, it seemed that they were related, the boy looked at the man with such love and admiration. The mother's smile too was full of adoration and familiarity."

Walter stopped and took my measure.

I had been shaking my head, lost in the picture of his dream. "What?"

"James, you'd better sit down."

I breathed a snicker at the irony. He was right; I'd been standing in the same position the whole time, one hand on my chin and my brow furrowed. I pulled up the nearest chair and settled into it.

What he described sounded like a scene from the Gospels. If I was right, the man in the center was Jesus of Nazareth, as described in the Scriptures, which I'd learned about in Sunday school as a boy. It shocked me to hear Walter describe the scene in his dream just as I had heard it in one of my most memorable Sunday school lessons.

Though I had attended church throughout my childhood, our lessons tended to avoid stories about Jesus's time on earth. But on this particular Sunday, my fifth grade class had a substitute teacher. A college girl, Sandy Schaefer, had agreed to fill in at the last minute. She said she didn't have time to prepare the lesson slated for that day, so she instead told us a story from the Gospels that she particularly liked.

This lesson stood out for me above all others from my Sunday school days. I suppose part of it was that a pretty, young woman, fresh and full of life, told the story. I had often thought of that story Sandy told us, reliving the soft buzz I felt sitting close to her in that small classroom. As she vividly told the Gospel story, I

And He Healed Them All

could see everything she described. The story she told and what she said about Jesus stood out in contrast to the endless tales of kings, prophets, and wars that were our usual syllabus.

Walter's dream seemed eerily similar.

"James, are you all right?" Walter broke into my reminiscence. "What is it that's got you so rattled?"

Again I breathed a laugh, self-consciously looking toward the window. "It's a story I heard once in Sunday school. I mean, I think your dream is about the same story in the Gospels that I heard when I was a kid in one particularly memorable Sunday school class."

Walter nodded. "Yes, I think it is about people gathering to see Jesus, or hear him teach. Maybe it was the feeding of the five thousand, or one of those stories."

"Yes, something like that." I agreed, though he seemed to be leaving out the part of the story that Sandy Schaefer thought the most important.

Walter sighed. "Do you know who the boy and woman are?"

"Not Jesus's wife and son." I smiled.

Walter laughed. "No, I didn't think that was who they were."

"Well, what happened next?" I rolled my hand to prompt him to continue.

"Oh, that was all. That was the end of the dream"

"Really? That seems a strange place to stop."

"I suppose. But isn't that the way with dreams? They seem to end at the most inopportune time. Maybe one of those night nurses trundled in and woke me out of my REM sleep just at that point."

I wondered if I should answer his question, and then he repeated it.

"Who do you think that woman and boy were?"

"Well, are you looking for the Freudian answer, or the one my Sunday school teacher would have given?"

"To hell with Freud, tell me the Sunday school version."

I took a deep breath and launched into the free fall of that memory. "Sandy Schaefer was a substitute teacher when I was ten years old. She taught us from her favorite Bible passage in the gospel of Matthew, I think. Despite the fact that we were all church kids, with parents established in our church, this story was completely new to us. It was the story of a large crowd gathering to see Jesus, to have him heal people and cast demons out of them, maybe even raise the dead. Of course, I don't remember the New Testament account. I'm only retelling what I remembered of Sandy's version.

"She told us that the crowd Jesus had famously fed with the few loaves and fish had gathered to be healed by him. The thing she kept coming back to was this phrase that I still remember after all these years: 'and he healed them all.'" I could still see her animated face, her wide-open eyes and arched thin brown eyebrows as I recalled this part.

A young nurse swept into the room. She wore a name tag that read *Tamarinda*. She came in to check on Walter's appetite. We both laughed when she told him they were serving fish for supper that night. I assembled a brief explanation for the laughter, and Walter welcomed the prospect of the meal.

When Tamarinda left, Walter picked up where we left off. "You say Jesus healed everyone in the crowd that he fed with that one boy's bread and fish?"

"That's the way Sandy Schaefer told it, and years later I think I did verify it."

"Who then were the woman and boy? Are they in the gospel story?"

"No, I don't think so. But I do remember that when one of us asked Sandy how all those people knew that Jesus would heal them, she told us that the Gospels frequently mentioned the way that news of Jesus's healing miracles caused crowds to gather wherever he went. It was even a problem for him, she'd said, because it made it impossible for him to go into large towns or cities. The crowds were too big and intense. That's why he resorted to meeting people out in rural places, like the hill in your dream. I think the woman was there because she or her son had been healed, and it was that miracle that brought the crowd. I don't know that for sure, of course. It's your dream, after all. But that's what popped into my head when you described the scene."

Walter adjusted his glasses on his thin nose. "So your teacher said that the crowds gathered to be healed? I guess I thought they just came to hear him teach. I knew I was seeing a sort of film version of a day in the life of Jesus. But I haven't ever stopped to think what it would have been like if he really did all of the miracles the Bible says he did." He stopped, tried to purse his lips with control over only half his mouth, apparently mulling some deep thought. "If your Sunday school teacher is right, I've been missing part of the story."

He stared down at the tumble of sheets and blankets cascaded over his inert form, but his steady gaze seemed to pass right through that concrete reality to somewhere his mind was wandering.

"The strangest thing is the way it all makes me feel," Walter said, looking over at me. I feel lighter, more hopeful than I have since the stroke."

"This must have been some dream to set you talking like that," I said.

"Oh, yes, it was quite a dream, indeed." He shifted in his bed, his voice still hollow with distraction.

I used the bed controls to help him sit up more. I plumped a pillow and replaced it behind his head.

Walter adjusted his blankets with his good hand. "It's made me hungrier than I've been in a long time. Just talking about it with you has given me an appetite." He laughed, evidently amused at himself.

Hope stirred within me that this one brief dream made such an impact on Walter, lifting his spirits and reviving his mind. Even if this dream was just the effect of an atrophied mind taking a few last swings, I drew courage from the change.

The rattle of the food cart stopped outside the door. Another nurse breezed into the room, carrying a white tray with Walter's fish dinner.

"Well, it looks like your feast has arrived," I said as I stood up. "Enjoy your supper."

"I will," he replied with a slanted grin.

I excused myself and said good-night to Walter, having stayed later than I expected. I checked my watch to see how late I was for meeting Jillian. It turned out that I was right on time. That venture into my deep, church-going past had obviously warped my sense of time.

I headed back down the quiet hall toward Jillian's office. I rounded the corner to her corridor and found her locking her door. She wore brown-rimmed glasses that made her look like a woman in an eyewear ad.

"Oh, I guess I'm a little late," I said, my head still full of Walter's story.

She smiled at me as she dropped her key into her briefcase. "No, just in time, I think."

I got lost in her smile for a moment.

"How's Walter tonight?" Jillian switched her briefcase to her other hand and turned to walk down the hallway. Her movement jarred me from my mental paralysis.

I walked alongside her. "He's doing okay. That is, I think he's okay." I held the front door for her.

"What do you mean?"

The cold hit me like a slap on the face. "Take my car?"

"Sure, but tell me about Walter."

"Well, he told me about a dream he had last night." I clicked the car remote and the flashing headlights punctuated my response.

"A disturbing dream?"

"Well, I'm a bit disturbed by it. But Walter seems excited."

"He's excited and you're disturbed?"

I opened the passenger door for her, and she slipped into the car.

By the time I got behind the wheel, I wondered whether it was polite to talk shop with Jillian, when she must have been ready to relax for the evening. "Do you want to talk about this now, or do you need some time to wind down a bit?"

She raised her eyebrows. "That's nice of you to ask. But I won't be able to wind down at all until you tell me about this dream."

I chuckled. Pulling out of the parking lot, I said, "Do you like Italian?"

"I do. But is this part of the dream?"

"No, this is the dinner part. I'm really not trying to tease you with the dream."

I glanced at her and caught the flash of a grin. She took off her glasses and slipped them into her briefcase. This reinforced my suspicion that the glasses were just part of her psychiatrist costume, never mind the hours her eyes spent with books, reports, and a computer screen.

I steered for my favorite Italian restaurant and told her about Walter's dream in as much detail as I could remember. She asked a few questions, like a good clinician and an interested listener. By the time we reached the restaurant I had finished the basic story.

"And you find this disturbing?" she said as we exited the car toward the ornate double doors of the restaurant.

I considered her question as we waited to be seated, the sultry sweet smell of wine, oregano and marinara sauce wrapping around us. Why was I so bothered by this dream? Walter loved it, and it did seem remarkable.

She studied me. "Maybe it's not the dream itself that's bothering you."

The hostess led us to a table in the back of the restaurant, swaying between the chairs in practiced rhythm, as if she could find our table with her eyes closed. The interruption offered another chance to think about what I was feeling.

We ordered drinks after we'd settled into our seats under a hanging Tiffany lamp, with an artificial candle flickering in the middle of the table. Once our waitress left, I picked up the conversation. "I suppose you're right. It's not the dream that bothers me as much as the whole process of watching Walter get old, and thinking about his death. Then this strange dream comes along and it's like a bright light in a dark place. It seems too good to be true, I guess."

"Too good to be true?" She tipped her head.

"I have a hard time adjusting to what I saw today. Last time I visited Walter, he looked so frail and lifeless. Then today he starts talking about this dream, and as he's telling it, he seems to look and act ten years younger. For a long time I've been dreading the final good-bye, then this dream invigorates him. It's like hope and inevitable loss are colliding in front of me."

Jillian nodded as she unwrapped her silverware from the black cloth napkin, apparently as eager for food as I was.

We sat back in our seats as the waitress delivered our drinks and took our dinner orders. Then Jillian picked up the topic again. "I've heard of things like this, even had patients with some fairly dramatic dreams that were life-giving experiences. It's as if they get close enough to the other side that they get a look through."

I furrowed my brow. "The other side?"

Jillian shrugged. "Sure, he's as near death as you assume. Maybe he's getting a glimpse of what comes next."

I looked at the yellow flicker of the fake candle reflected in her eyes. "So, you believe in . . . heaven . . . and life after death?" I shifted in my seat, pulling my legs under me.

"I've seen too many things not to believe." She sipped her drink and looked me square in the eyes. It wasn't exactly a challenge, but that look left no room for uncertainty about how she felt.

I realized I had succumbed to stereotyping, assuming this attractive psychiatrist was a modern intellectual who would naturally reject such notions as spiritually significant dreams. I scolded myself.

"Why not just welcome the change in Walter?" She turned it back on me.

I nodded. "Good question. Why not, indeed?"

The waitress setting our salads before us served as a segue to lighter conversation. I learned about Jillian's family and her work. We meandered from the predictable and safe topics to pathways leading deeper into the uncertain parts of our lives, less safe parts.

Jillian had caught me deep in doubt and distrust about Walter's amazing dream, yet she trusted me with her concerns about her ailing mother, her self-doubt about the pressures of her work among the elderly, so lonely and ailing and close to death. I guess that's what endeared her to me so early. That she could see my flaws, the bits of paint missing, the dents and substituted parts, and yet she still trusted me with her heart.

I dropped Jillian off at the nursing home and waited to make sure her car would start on that icy winter night.

As I waited, I determined to visit Walter on Sunday. Not only to see how he was feeling, but I wanted another shot at connecting with him and his dream experience.

I followed Jillian out of the parking lot. My tires slipped and then caught on dry pavement. As I turned the opposite direction from Jillian, my headlights melted the solid darkness just enough for me to squeeze through.

Chapter Two
Lightning Strikes Twice

That Sunday morning, I slept late, took time to make a really good pot of coffee, and sat in my favorite rocking chair to read the newspaper. For the first time in years, however, I gave a thought to missing church on a Sunday morning. It was just a thought, not a commitment to do anything about it.

I had grown tired of the same old church experience that bored me when I was a child, only modernized a bit to cater to a contemporary audience. It was one of the things Debra and I argued about. She liked the clubishness of her church, the bake sales, and other fund-raisers, and she liked the head of marketing, also known as the pastor. To me it all seemed reduced to the lowest common denominator, so I checked out.

On Sunday I could take a leisurely approach to the morning, in contrast to hustling off to classes or committee meetings all week, even some Saturdays. The mental stress of trying not to criticize the weak arguments and rah-rah presentation of the churches I had attended wasn't restful, wasn't healthy. At least, that's what I told myself.

Me and *The Times*, that's all I wanted on a Sunday morning.

Later that afternoon I made the ten-minute drive to see Walter. Sunday was a popular day to visit, so the halls were active with people of various ages, many dressed for church and pushing someone in a wheelchair or walking very slowly next to a self-propelled elder with a walker or cane. I stood in the middle of the wide hall for half a minute while one balding, middle-aged man

And He Healed Them All

coaxed a much older woman past Walter's door.

"C'mon, Ma. I think you're in somebody's way here," he said, a bit too harshly for my sensibilities.

I forced a fake smile, like a dog trying to fit a small Frisbee into his mouth.

Walter was sitting up already when I knocked on his door and pushed it open.

"It happened again," Walter said as soon as he saw me step in. "I was back there again. They were all pressing toward him, all of them who could stand on their own, that is."

He throttled back from giddy to instructive, and I pulled up a chair.

"So you had the same dream?"

"No, not the same dream; a continuation of the first dream, like the next part of the story."

Chills skittered up my spine. I shook my head, speechless.

Walter smiled at me, a paternal stare over the top of his glasses, clearly enjoying my surprise. Seeing him staring like that, I cracked a smile as well. His mood was contagious. But mostly I was curious about the vigor and intensity with which Walter addressed me. His transformation from before the first dream almost startled me.

"You seem to be feeling better," I said.

He nodded. "Quite a bit better, actually."

"Well, tell me."

He raised his eyebrows at my urgency, but settled quickly into his role as narrator.

"The crowd looked like people at a wedding, standing as the bride enters. Or people beside a parade ogling their favorite celebrity . . . that is, until you looked into their eyes. It wasn't just excitement, I saw pain too. It was as if they were so filled with hope and expectation that it hurt. Most eyes were full of tears, but not necessarily tears of sadness.

"And in the center was that man again. His eyes were the most remarkable thing about him. They were alert, probing, as if he was looking for something and finding it then still looking for more." He took in a shaky breath. "All that at once is the best way I can describe him."

I shook my head, more at Walter's animated account than the content of what he was saying. I'd never seen him this enlivened in all our years of friendship. I knew that Walter faithfully attended his Presbyterian church, but I never heard him speak so excitedly about a Bible story.

He tapped the bed control, indicating he wanted to sit up more. As I'd done many times before, I elevated his bed and situated his pillows to make him more comfortable. Neither of us acknowledged the awkwardness of two academics struggling with sheets and pillows as if we were in a hurry to go somewhere.

Walter tugged at his pajamas with his one good hand to try to undo a twist. He gave up, so I tried to fix it, until I saw Walter's eyes shift left and right, as if looking for a way out of the awkwardness.

"Tell me about the dream." I stepped back and sank into the chair.

He grinned that sort of three-quarters smile the stroke had left him. "You were right about the woman and the boy, I could tell from their conversation that she was a widow with only the one son to support her in her old age, though she was not what we would call old at all."

Walter's confident tone and relaxed demeanor told me that he had been thinking a lot about the dream, such that recalling it was easy.

Walter reached for a cup of water with his left hand. "It's strange. The people in that crowd were almost all standing like they had been waiting in line for the bathroom for a long time." He chuckled at his own analogy. "But the remarkable thing was that the teacher didn't seem in any hurry. He smiled at them, his eyes full of peace."

Walter snorted another laugh. "His disciples, this little group of bodyguards, were another story altogether. They all looked annoyed with the crowd. I could see their tensed jaws and vigilant glances. For the most part, they reminded me of policemen assigned to crowd control, their eyes searching the faces of the people pushing around them, or staring above the crowd as if they were so many cattle. I guess my impression was that they had done this before."

Walter looked squarely at me. "You know, this dream is almost better than actually being there. If I were really there, I would've had to ask dozens of questions to learn half of what I could observe in this sort of out-of-body presence."

He stared at window. At times, as he continued narrating the dream, I wondered if he remembered that I was even in the room.

"This amazing crowd included groups of people who despised one another. I could tell that there were some long-standing differences among them: rich and poor, Jew and Gentile, people from regions near and far. I could see the suspicion in the narrowed eyes of a small group of Samaritans as Jews from nearby Jerusalem surrounded them. Disgust twisted the faces of Jews who bumped up against Romans. The children just stared at all the strangers who would likely never have bothered to come into their little villages.

"I suppose it was a sign of their desperation that these parochial people would put up with the mixed crowd they found themselves in. For me, not affiliated with anyone in that crowd, it was simply a marvelous oddity to see the array of cultures and hear the various dialects and languages. Yes, I could understand what they were saying, as if they all spoke English, but as is the way of dreams, I knew at the same time that they were not speaking any language I understood.

"Anyway, these people pressed toward the top of the hill, held at bay by the bulwark of men guarding the teacher. The bodyguards held their ground, in spite of people pushing at them and shouting over their heads, calling out requests for help, cries for healing for themselves or for friends or family they'd brought with them. Apparently the people at the front had diseases or injuries that didn't prevent them from pushing past hundreds of others to reach the front of the mob.

"Inside the small enclave, the teacher stepped up on a half-

And He Healed Them All

buried boulder and raised his hands to silence the crowd. As though he were a choir director with a well-trained chorus, they all became instantly quiet—not totally silent, of course, but enough to hear his voice ring out over them.

"He didn't strike me as a remarkable man in terms of his physical appearance. But his bearing commanded the attention of everyone. When he stood up on that rock, I imagine most of the people were seeing him for the first time.

"I think I can recall most of his words. He said, 'Brothers and sisters, I know that you have come to be healed today. And you will not be disappointed. But I must ask you to be patient so that all who are in need can be taken care of in good time. Please be aware of those around you, and be careful not to hurt one another. There are already plenty of things to heal here without causing further injury to anyone.'

"Many laughed when he said this, but I think it was mostly relief inspired by his promise that they would not be disappointed. Once the laughter died down, he continued.

"'Follow the directions of my friends here as they lead you to where I can touch you and again as they lead you away. They will help you and will answer any questions you may have.'

"At this I saw at least one of his disciples look at him with a scowl. I wondered whether he had made this assurance as a sort of tease to them, but that wasn't clear to me.

"The crowd seemed to settle into his instructions, but only for a few seconds. Soon after he stepped down from his perch on that boulder, a disturbance began working its way through the clot of people near the top of that hill. Insane noises emanated from a swirling current in the crowd, with people exclaiming and cursing in return as they were tossed aside to make way for a circus-like formation of men plowing through. As the disturbance neared the circle of the teacher's friends, one who had been holding back the crowd shouted and backed away in shock. Another raised his fist as though to beat back the intruders, but he just stood in stunned stillness at the sight before him.

"A man, no more than a hundred thirty pounds, thrashed,

cursed, and spat as four burly men dragged him by ropes. Leather straps had been buckled to the man, intended to protect him from the ropes cutting into him, I expect, though in more than one place I could see redness that warned of deep lacerations if this struggle continued.

"The teacher pushed through his friends while the onlookers spilled back to stay clear of the mad man's flailing arms and legs. The four men restraining him appeared to be Gentiles, dark skinned, perhaps from points west, such as Egypt or Libya. The small man they were attempting to contain seemed to be from no earthly place. His eyes bulged impossibly wide so that they were nearly entirely exposed. His face was so dark red as to be nearly black, though his captors did not seem to be strangling him in any way. I felt profound terror when I saw this. Even though I knew I wasn't physically there. I felt fear deep inside, as if that horrid man was transmitting it, as if he broadcast fear when he spun and kicked.

"The teacher stepped up to the captive and spoke sharply, but with no hint of fear or panic. 'Stop!' He said, as if commanding a misbehaving dog.

"At his command, the man stopped thrashing and stood dead still, his wild eyes locked on the eyes of the teacher. As they stood face-to-face, the man's countenance changed remarkably. His color faded to nearly normal and his eyes became human and no longer protruded so bizarrely. It was like the shadow of a cloud passed, allowing the sun to shine through. But then the madness returned, doubly intense. The madman tossed his four captors violently, two of the ropes snapped and the other two were wrenched from the captors' hands. The lunatic seemed to levitate as he screamed and thrashed.

"Through all this, standing before him, unmoved, the teacher kept his eyes fixed on the insane man. Again he issued a simple command. 'Come out of him right now.' He spoke not to the man, but to the cloud that seemed to shroud him. Again it left him. But this time the man fell flat on his face as if tackled from behind. He lay perfectly still.

"People in the crowd looked around, as if searching for the one who had knocked him unconscious like that. Was it the teacher, or one of the men who had dragged him there?

"After a moment, the man got to his hands and knees; then he pulled himself up so that he knelt before the teacher. He rubbed the back of his hand across his eyes, wiping away tears. He began speaking like a man in full charge of his wits. 'I left my wife and child years ago. A growing madness was stealing my life. I lost my job. I feared that, in my rage, I would harm my wife and son, so I left to protect them and to try to find work in nearby towns, where my reputation for a violent temper was unknown.' He fell to his face again before the teacher. 'I miss my family!'

"'Help him to his feet,' the teacher said. One of his brawny keepers bent down to take the arm of the prone man, who stirred, and then raised himself to his hands and knees again.

"Finally, he stood before the teacher, though he hung his head and slumped his shoulders. 'I lived like a dog, totally out of my mind.' He raised his eyes and looked into the gentle face of the teacher.

"The former lunatic fell into the embrace of his deliverer. The teacher whispered into the man's ear. I couldn't hear what he said. But the man listened intently, like someone receiving detailed instructions from a mentor and friend. He nodded as he stepped back and received the approving smile of the healer, offering emphatic thanks.

"The man turned and began to push his way patiently, but persistently, through the crowd. 'I'm going home! I'm going to see my wife and child!'

"The crowd parted. Some patted him on the back as he passed. But mostly they watched silently as the liberated man slipped past them. They stood breathless for just a moment, recovering from the fear the demented man had stirred. Then, as if communicating wordlessly from one end of the crowd to the other, the people turned and surged toward the teacher. However, they didn't threaten to crush the teacher and his friends, rather they leaned in, like obedient children restraining their excitement over a gift they're about to receive.

"The teacher addressed a woman I hadn't noticed before. 'Leah,' he said to her. Her eyes widened and her mouth formed an O at hearing her name. She was clearly startled that he knew it. Then he spoke to someone else, or something else. He used words I couldn't understand, as if in some language that my dream couldn't translate. Instantly, Leah screamed as if stabbed with pain. Then she fell silent, standing and holding on to the extended arms of the teacher, steadying herself. She laughed, and her laughter splashed onto those near her and in turn to those beyond them, until hundreds of people laughed together, a great relieved laughter of people bonded together in an emotional trauma, still recovering from the demented man's display, I expect.

"The teacher released her, and she wobbled a moment, until she put her arms around a man next to her. He looked on her in adoration then spoke to the teacher. 'Thank you, teacher. I brought my wife in hopes that you would heal her of the headaches that had bent and broken her daily.' He laughed and cried. He put his arm around his wife and turned to leave.

"The teacher caught hold of his arm, preventing him from fully turning away. 'And what would you have me do for you?'

"As if surprised to find that he had an answer to that question, he replied. 'My ear; I can't hear—'

"The teacher cupped the husband's left ear with one hand.

"A second later, the man jerked away from the teacher's touch as if he'd received an electric shock. His face brightened. He covered his other ear and reported. 'I can hear. I can hear out of this ear now!'

"To the teacher's right, a few of his friends, including two women, were helping those who couldn't stand. Stretcher-bearers lowered their charges to the ground in rows so that the teacher had room to move between the crippled and seriously ill who lay there awaiting his attention. I hadn't noticed those women before or that more than the twelve men comprised his security crew. The helpers, both men and women, moved automatically, as if familiar with their tasks, only sparse communication among them. They arranged broken and withered bodies while uttering reassurances and giving orders alternately. They reminded me of hospital personnel, trying to strike a balance between professional efficiency and personal compassion.

"As I think about it now, the teacher always seemed to have a clear idea about what to do next. Before him stood a multitude of people with a wide variety of needs. They leaned toward him, longing for immediate help; however, it seemed he had an agenda. Though maybe agenda isn't the right word; at least he seemed to know what he wanted to do next. He didn't always simply turn to the next person in line; rather, he seemed to choose someone he wanted to touch or speak to.

"At one point in the wall of people before him, four women stood together, clutching one another like people on a wildly rocking boat, though they stood on solid, stony ground. They stared at the teacher as if he were a dangerous animal. Others around them were calling out, some even pushing forward. But these four—who clearly had arrived early enough to establish a front place in the crowd—now seemed to shrink back. The teacher held out his hands as he approached them. They eyed his hands.

"'Sisters, which of you is sick?' When none answered, he tried again. 'Who is the one called Rachel?'

"At that, they stepped back slightly into the forest of humanity pushing in behind them. But one hesitated, not pulling back as quickly as the others. I figured she must be Rachel.

"All four of these women must have been attractive at one time, but now they looked hard, like they'd lived a rough life that had scarred them. They wore the look of abused women: eyes downcast, heads slightly turned as if checking for an escape route. The one called Rachel looked feverish, even haggard; her long hair straggled out of her sweat-stained head covering. Her hollow eyes and furrowed brows conveyed a silent desperation.

"The teacher stepped up to her and touched her face. He stroked her forehead and then cupped her cheek. Rachel fell to the ground, as though she'd fainted. Her three companions gasped. The teacher knelt and helped her sit up. He looked from Rachel up to the three other women. 'Yes, I know who you are, and what you do to earn bread and a place to sleep. I know this disease is a curse of your profession. And I know who you are beyond what you do.'

"His words seemed to break through their defenses. They began to weep uncontrollably. The teacher kissed the forehead of Rachel before standing up. Again, she fell back as if in a faint. While she lay at his feet, he touched each of the three other women on the shoulder or forehead. He seemed to be blessing them in some way. They continued to weep.

"Rachel began to stir and gathered herself to stand. She dusted off her clothing and then, with the help of her friends, stood. She stared down at her once colorful garments. She quickly wrapped her outer cloak around her. It wasn't a cold day, but she seemed to be trying to conceal the gaudy clothing of her profession. I smiled because her action demonstrated modesty, probably something she and her friends hadn't considered for years. She gestured, as if trying to find words with her hands. Finally, she spoke, her eyes wide with discovery. 'I'm well. I feel so much better. I am healed!' She declared it for all to hear.

"At that point, I noticed that those standing immediately around the women had pulled back from the healed prostitute. Some scowled in her direction and whispered among themselves while shaking their heads. I overheard things like, 'Could this be right, for the teacher to heal such as these? Could this be from God?' Then I understood that Rachel was declaring something she was sure others wouldn't believe she deserved.

"That's when I spotted a rabbi, a synagogue teacher. The smallish man with long, gray-streaked whiskers wore a black head covering characteristic of his office. He stood among the skeptics. He shook his head, watching the teacher, glowering with pursed lips. He made a move as if to turn away but stopped when the teacher approached him directly and interrupted his retreat. The teacher cocked his head slightly to one side when their eyes met, as if examining the other man's reaction and waiting for the religious leader to utter his conclusions.

"The rabbi finally spoke. 'The way you healed that woman . . . and blessed the other three is expressly forbidden. They are unclean. The Law says that anyone who touches an unclean thing is therefore also unclean.'

"The teacher nodded slightly but asked a question. 'And what would you have me do for you? I know that you had concluded I am a prophet from God, and my healing power comes from God. But now you question it because I touched and healed these women.'

"If I was surprised that the teacher knew the thoughts of the rabbi, the religious man must have been doubly amazed, for he opened his mouth to speak, yet nothing came out. The rabbi closed his gaping mouth, shook his head again, and clenched and unclenched his fists.

"The teacher stepped closer to him. He peered deeply into the old man's eyes, as though searching for something. 'You can no longer read the Scriptures. You came here to ask for your sight to be restored.'

"'How do you know about me?'

"The teacher watched the rabbi back away. He glanced briefly toward the sky and nodded. 'You don't have to resign yourself to dependence on students reading to you, to no longer exercise the rabbi's greatest privilege of reading the Torah for himself.'

"The rabbi stopped dead in his tracks, tottered for a moment, and almost fell over. He reached out with both hands, as if feeling for something to grab hold of. At first, I thought that perhaps he had suddenly been struck blind, that God had punished him in response to his rejection of the teacher. He staggered and squinted. Then his eyes grew wide and he swung his head first one way then the other. He held his wrinkled old hand in front of his face, turning it front to back. He seemed fascinated with it. He broke into a smile. Then he spun back toward the teacher.

"By then the teacher was holding the head of an old man and seemed to be speaking into the top of it. The rabbi watched as the old man suddenly straightened, let out a small cry, and looked at the teacher. 'I can see! The fogginess is gone. I can see!' He raised his hands toward heaven and shouted, 'Glory to God in the highest!'

"The teacher looked toward the rabbi and raised his eyebrows.

"The rabbi stepped closer, shaking his head slightly, his new eyes wide open under his bushy eyebrows. He hesitated a moment and then turned to walk away. As he resumed his path, he bumped into a woman who was dancing joyously, lost in praising God. The rabbi stumbled and then regained his balance. The young woman stopped her dance to check that she had not injured the older man. Their eyes met. Eye-to-eye with the rabbi stood the prostitute, Rachel. She breathed a sigh, perhaps that she hadn't hurt the old rabbi, or maybe she let go of some kind of emotional burden. As for the rabbi, he turned back to his path, but this time with a small straight smile.

"I don't know what he would have thought about the next healing, however, for a tax collector stepped forward to be healed, a well-dressed collaborator with Rome, taking money from Israel that should have gone to a Jewish king and to the temple. Certainly, the rabbi would have thought this tax collector as unclean as those prostitutes.

"The tax collector told the teacher his name was Jacob. He held his stomach, his pale face pinched as if in great pain. In fact, he paused for a moment and vomited blood onto the ground in front of the teacher. The teacher pursed his lips and waited for the tax collector to wipe his mouth with a rag that was stained with blood and bile. Weakened, Jacob fell to his knees.

"The teacher patted Jacob's cheek gently and then reached down for his stomach. He declared, with authority, like a command to the stomach. 'Restoration!'

"The tax collector groaned and then drew in a tremendous breath. Healthy color infused Jacob's face, which had suddenly softened. His breathing eased. He stood and then hesitated, as if checking himself. He seemed convinced that he wasn't going to be sick. His matted and tangled beard flexed, as a wide grin stretched across his face. 'Thank you, sir. Thank you, so much. God bless you.'

"The teacher nodded to him before moving to help another, a boy leaning on a crutch. Without asking about the problem, the teacher bent down and touched the boy's leg. Instantly the boy made a little hop, as if he had stepped on something sharp. A smile lighted the boy's face. The teacher ruffled his hair. He was about to say something but was interrupted.

"A middle-aged man with stark white hair growled. At first, it seemed funny to me, a grown man making animal noises like a child. The growling was as uninhibited as a child's game, but this was no little boy.

"'Stop that!' The teacher spoke sharply.

"The man stopped suddenly, as if the teacher had insulted him. The teacher grabbed the man's head in both hands and made a little growling noise of his own, or maybe it was just a low guttural prayer. Either way, the white-haired man's eyes popped wide open. 'I can hear. I can hear!' He put both hands to his head. 'The headaches, they're gone! And I feel clean inside.'

"Around him, the crowd rippled with murmurs as they pointed to him. His white hair had changed to a more natural black and gray.

"The sun had arched well up in the sky by this time, warming the barren hillside. Only the slightest hint of a breeze muted the Mediterranean heat. Those accompanying the sick provided shade for them, and youngsters were sent down the hill for water. There was, of course, no provision for this many people so far from any town.

"Off to the right of the teacher, a disturbance stirred the crowd. I don't think the teacher saw it, because he was busy restoring the flexibility to a man's elbow. Shouting, cursing, and a cloud of dust rose about ten yards from where the teacher stood. A moment later the crowd parted and a man appeared, holding another man by the collar and hitting him when he tried to break away.

"'Peter!' the teacher said.

And He Healed Them All

"Peter, a leather-skinned man with a hard brow and lively eyes, stopped hitting the man but kept his grip on the thin, wolfish man with a pointed beard. 'This thief was cutting purse strings and picking things out of people's bags and baskets.' Peter scowled at the thief. The men around him hemmed in the thief when they heard this, so that Peter had to struggle less forcefully to keep the thief in custody.

"The teacher stepped into the space directly in front of the captive, whose eyes were downcast, fixed on the ground. First the teacher spoke to Peter. 'Did you return what he stole?'

"'As much as I saw him steal.'

"The teacher nodded, keeping his eyes on the man the whole time. The thief raised his head and looked at the teacher. I wondered if he was checking for a way to escape, but once he met the eyes of the teacher he remained still. His tangled hair had acquired a patina of dust, presumably from the scuffle with Peter. He must have been knocked to the ground at least once, and looked the worse for it. The teacher wiped the man's face and put his finger on a long, ugly scar running from above his right eyebrow past the corner of his mouth. The jagged line subtly distorted the shape of the thief's face.

"Those two men now seemed oblivious to the crowd around them. The teacher traced the scar from top to bottom. The features of the hard, angry face of the captive thief turned into the frightened face of a child. He burst into tears. Peter let go of the thief's coat; but the teacher maintained his gentle touch on the man's face.

"The teacher spoke just above a whisper. 'Those who hurt you will hurt you no more. Those that haunt you will haunt you no more. Your Father in heaven heals you and welcomes you into his household.'

"With that, the teacher pulled back his hand. The disfiguring scar was gone. All that remained were tear tracks through the dust. The thief opened his eyes and looked again into the teacher's. He reached for his belt and pulled a pouch from under his cloak, turning slightly to hand this to Peter.

"Peter glanced at the teacher, shrugged, and then went back through the crowd, apparently to try to sort out who had lost this remaining contraband.

"As I looked on, it felt as if the two men, the teacher and the former thief, remained locked in a mental connection, like links in a chain.

"I wondered if this bonding had some healing power in itself. To be attended to so truly and purely, to have the complete and total attention of one so caring and compassionate must have powerfully affected these people as did the physical healing they received, of course."

Walter stopped there, his head slightly bowed, a content smile bending his lips.

"That was the end?" I said.

"I think so." Walter squinted, as if to see into his tired old memory. "I'm sure I left things out, but it seems to me that's about where it ended."

"Doesn't seem like an ending does it?" I said.

He gave me the same sly smile that he used to show to students who were close to getting an important point he was making in class. I had seen that look a hundred times and felt an internal shift into an undefined hope, at least a hope that wasn't clear to me at that point. I remained conflicted about the dreams, still trying to convince myself that this experience was real.

"You know, I think the best part of this experience is seeing the face of Jesus," Walter said, as if hearing my thoughts. "The look in his eyes when he sees someone in need makes me desperate to believe that what I'm seeing is real. 'Cause if it is real, and this is actually what Jesus was like, then he deserves a lot more from me than a sort of passive acceptance and bit of attention during a brief hour on Sunday."

I rubbed my Sunday whiskers, neglected by the razor for my day of rest. My own response to that challenge Walter saw in the dreams remained under layers and layers of accumulated questions and missing answers. I didn't feel as if I could even begin to dig out of my unbelief far enough to consider the leap of faith

Walter seemed to be contemplating.

    When I didn't say anything, he said, "I think there's more in this for you and me. It's not over yet."

Chapter Three
Going Deeper

I called Jillian at home after leaving Walter on Sunday. We agreed to meet at a coffee shop near campus after work the next day.

The cool, dark street backed our reflection in the front window next to table where we sat. Two people over forty, perhaps slimmer than average, bookish, and mostly serious, looked at each other across a white Melamine table and over steaming cups that warmed slightly red noses. This was the first time I'd seen her without her hair pinned up and her therapist attire. She wore a different pair of glasses that made her look younger, almost like one of my students, though she was certainly twice the age of those college kids.

I put both hands between my knees in search of warmth and looked from her blurred reflection in the window to her live presence. "Anything remarkable at work today?" I realized too late how much it sounded like something I would have asked Debra when we were still married.

Jillian nodded. "A woman I'd been caring for died early this morning." She looked at me as if to assess the impact of her news, as aware as I was of how different that workplace experience was from anything I faced at school.

I sighed slightly and pursed my lips. "How are you doing with that?"

She smiled and studied me, as if she were weighing some kind of complex proposal. "Thanks for asking." She looked down at her sugar-free mocha. "Alice, the woman who died, was suffering from dementia for the last years of her life, and I felt like I lost contact with her months ago, as if she was gone from her frail, old body already. That makes her death seem sort of like the end of a mourning process instead of the beginning. But then, it makes everything seem so final. Any little hope of improvement, even for a glimpse of clarity, is over now."

"How do you do it? How do you face the loss and suffering day in and day out?"

She shook her head. "I hope it doesn't sound like a religious dodge, but for me God gives grace for just what we need. It may seem impossible to you, but that's just because you're not called to it. I have to grieve, but I know from experience that life and hope lie at the end of every grieving experience."

I shook my head in wonder at the woman seated across from me. Her hair was pushed behind her ears but some of her rich locks slipped off of her left shoulder in a big loop. I felt the need to set my emotional emergency brake right there and then. I so admired everything I had observed in Jillian to that point that a moment of panic warned me to slow way down internally. Externally, I hoped I looked like I was just sitting in that body-molded plastic chair, stirring my latte.

Perhaps picking up the sound of my internal alerts, Jillian asked one of those hard questions. "How long have you been divorced?"

Most people avoid the "D" topic, though anyone with any prospect of a romantic attachment knows they have to traverse that territory some time. I admired her courage (along with everything else).

"Six, no, five years." I recalculating even as I rewarded her courage with a ready answer. I smiled, knowing what she should ask next. "And, yes, I'm over it, if being over it means no longer lying awake at night replaying the arguments, the negotiations with lawyers, and the things I wish I would have said all along the way. I sleep fine now, and without the aid of medication."

"I've had those nights," she said, quick to let me know that this was not a doctor-patient conversation. "I was engaged twice. The first was when I was in college and the second was four years ago. I remember those replayed arguments, and even just recalled conversations where I would have said it better if I had just had a chance to script it ahead of time." She sipped her mocha.

I watched every detail of her movements. "I tried the scripting thing, writing these long, insightful emails late at night when I was so sure they would fix everything. That was a failure every time."

She laughed. "You mean I've been deceiving myself all this time? The script doesn't help?"

I nodded, trying to look the wise old sage.

After finishing our warm drinks and some less weighty conversation, we parted that night, each driving our own vehicles, with mutual confidence, I think, that we would be seeing each other again and not just in Walter's room at the retirement home.

On the following Wednesday, I had barely entered Walter's room when he announced, "I had another dream!"

"A new episode?" I said, half joking.

He laughed. "Yes. It was clearly a continuation of the first two. Sit. Let me tell you what I remember of the dream." He pointed to the chair.

As I pulled off my coat and sank into the chair, I said, "I've gotta get you a digital recorder in case this goes on like this."

"That might be a good idea," Walter said. "All set?"

I nodded once.

Walter started, in the even and warm storytelling tone I learned to expect of his dream narrations.

"I saw a little girl standing in front of the teacher; her face was horribly scarred."

As Walter told his dream, I closed my eyes and tried to picture it.

"Her mother said, 'She fell into a fire when she was small. Doctors had done all they could to get the skin to heal back over her chin and nose. It causes her continuous pain. Can you help her?'

"'*Can* I?' The teacher raised his eyebrows. He smiled.

"Kneeling down he took the girl's face in his big hands. He looked at her. 'Like new,' is all he said.

"The girl jumped back as if he had pinched her. But he still cupped his hands as if around her face. Any thought that the teacher might have hurt the girl in some way vanished with the look on her face. She beamed. Her skin was smooth and clean, as it was meant to be. She was completely restored.

"'Alleluia!' she shouted.

"Her mother joined in praising God, only she didn't stop with just one word.

"The girl jumped up into her mother's arms.

"While mother and daughter rejoiced, the teacher went to a man with the bottom part of his left leg missing; the stump stuck out in front as he stood between two wooden crutches.

"'How did this happen?'

"'When I was a boy, I was working in the field with my older brother. I stumbled under the oxen when I tried to grab at a butterfly that flew in front of the plow. My brother shouted at me and tried to stop the plow, but it was too late. The plow raked over my leg.' The man struggled to speak, shaking like an animal in shock.

"'Whose fault was it?'

"The man looked puzzled, as if to wonder what difference it would make. 'Mine, I suppose.' His voice vibrated with his shaking.

"The teacher nodded. 'We should forgive that little boy, shouldn't we?'

"The man cocked his eyebrows, obviously surprised at the thought. 'Yes, I suppose.'

"The teacher said no more. He reached for the stump of the man's leg. I can only describe what followed as resembling someone forming a leg and a foot out of clay. The teacher took hold of the stump and it seemed to grow in his hand. It took nearly a minute of forming and stretching. The whole time, the man shouted over and over, as if someone was poking him with a sharp stick.

"The woman and her daughter who had been healed from the burn scar had stayed to see what the teacher would do next. They began to shout and dance and sing their Alleluias again. Others around them followed in the song. Meanwhile, the man with the new leg held his crutches above his head and spun around and around, singing and shouting praises to God, until he was too dizzy to stand. Two of the teacher's friends caught the unsteady man as he fell over laughing.

"The teacher stood, closed his eyes briefly, and raised his face to the sky, as if simply enjoying the heat of the sun on his skin. He touched the out-stretched hand of one of the singers, who stopped his song and reached inside his shirt to feel along his collarbone. 'It's gone! The sore lump has disappeared. Alleluia!'

"In another moment, a woman who had come with a raw-looking rash on her face was on the ground, crying tears of joy at her healing. She kept stroking her silky cheeks and neck as she cried and shouted praises along with the growing chorus of worshippers around her.

"The teacher's healing touch seemed to gravitate toward the worshippers. Men waving their hands above their heads to celebrate the healings they witnessed received his touch and grabbed the parts of their bodies that had been sick or wounded but were now healed. Smiles, shouts, and laughter followed.

"It was hard to understand what they were all saying because of the shouting and laughing that layered over the singing. The worship was purely spontaneous. The people seemed unable to stop themselves. And the energy of their thanksgiving seemed to feed the hand of the healer with more power. He no longer stopped to talk to the people he touched; he simply healed them and moved on to the next person. Many of those he touched fell backward or lurched forward.

"Reaching for one man while looking at a young woman he apparently intended to heal next, the teacher received a kick under his bearded chin when the man screamed and flipped backward, his feet a full five feet off the ground before he hit the

And He Healed Them All

dirt. The teacher stumbled back into the arms of his friends, who were never far behind him. He regained his footing quickly while holding his chin. The worship faltered briefly and then swelled as he laughed at the joke he had played on himself.

"The next person he touched, he made a playful point of reaching out while holding his face back out of harm's way. His smile made it clear that he was teasing.

"The woman whose withered hand he healed thrust her fully restored hand in the air and shouted praise with a liberated howl. Other healthy hands waved in the air to echo the thanksgiving. Grateful for their healing, the people began to dance and sing, joining the whirl of worshippers who trailed the healing teacher like the churning wake of a boat.

"At this point, an older man came forward with the help of a young woman. His head was swathed in cloth, only a hint of gleaming eyes visible in the dark cave formed by this covering. I heard the young woman say to the teacher amidst the joyous din, 'My father.' The rest of what she said was lost in the tumult. The teacher stood squarely before the man, peering at the strange figure. The father responded slowly. Gingerly, with just the tips of his fingers, he unwound the cloth.

"What he revealed halted the nearby swirl of worship. Several people gasped. More than one woman stifled a scream with her hands to her mouth. A heavy hush fell over the crowd. Several people stepped back, as if fearing the man's ailment might be contagious. I've seen pictures of this dreaded affliction. The father apparently suffered from some sort of parasite like that which produces elephantiasis. His face was grossly swollen and distorted. Though nearly normal on one side, it was grotesquely enlarged on the other. The eye on the swollen side was only a dark point hidden deep in what had been his cheek and forehead. His breath rasped hoarsely from his twisted mouth, his neck and throat distorted by the disease.

"The teacher leaned forward with a fierce look, like a lion protecting his cub. The man and his daughter seemed dumbstruck by the piercing focus the teacher drilled into the gruesome face. The teacher appeared to look through the distorted mask, and with clenched fists he commanded, 'Come out of him, now!'

"This was the most force I had heard the teacher express. It was a command that one dared not disobey. The hair on my neck bristled. At first the ailing man stood perfectly still, but within seconds, he started to twist back and forth. My experience suddenly became more dreamlike to me, because I saw a change on the suffering man's face that I can't explain naturally. It was as if, for a second, the face of a dreadfully suffering child was imposed over the face of the diseased man. The ghost-like face of the child flashed in and out several times. Because of the moans and gasps from people standing near him, I realized they were likely seeing some part of this as well.

"Then the father stumbled forward, falling onto his hands and knees. His daughter stood next to him, with both of her hands over her mouth. She seemed frozen, unable to move or speak. The teacher reached down and held the back of the man's head with one hand, while his other hand clenched. I was horrified when the teacher swung his fist and struck the man in the back of the head. He struck him, not softly, not hesitantly, but with power that caused the already struggling man to buckle and fall to his face.

"After a moment, water poured from the man's face as he slowly pressed himself back up to his hands and knees. It was more fluid than either sweat or tears could account for. He coughed, and more water gushed from his mouth.

"The teacher still stood with one hand on the man's head, his other no longer raised, but relaxed at his side. He waited as the man remained on his hands and knees, facing the ground, silent, as if recovering from the trauma of the healing process, for indeed he was healed. He glanced up at the teacher, his face as normal as yours or mine.

"The young woman helped her father to his feet. He wiped at his face with his sleeve, mopping away some of the remaining moisture. Women screamed and men shouted in amazement. One woman stepped forward and looked as if she wanted to grab the healed man's face in her hands. She seemed barely able to restrain herself, standing close and staring into the handsome face.

"The man returned a brief glancing smile, his head slightly bowed. He swung his attention back to the teacher, looking at him with such love and thanksgiving. And the teacher looked deeply into the man's now bright eyes. The healer put his right hand to the side of the face that had once been so swollen and distorted. The man's hand followed. He tenderly felt his own cheek, chin and neck, and he smiled again at the teacher.

"The teacher said to him, 'Trust God to keep you free; don't be afraid of anything, not past, present, or future.'

"The man nodded then turned to his daughter, whose face was wetter than his. Tears washed down her cheeks as she embraced him. She gasped and then sobbed some more.

"Worship had spun into the air once again, dancers and singers raising hands and voices to the sky to praise God for his goodness and mercy. Robes billowed like bells as men and women twirled in spontaneous dance. High-pitched voices warbled above the washing wave of open song.

"The teacher bent to speak to a hunchbacked woman and touched her stooped back, briefly closing his eyes. Several people pushed toward the teacher, evidently eager to be the next beneficiary to this amazing healing. The teacher's friends formed a tightened circle around him and pressed back against the crowd. To the right of where the teacher stood, I heard a cry of pain and a scuffle, accompanied by swearing and accusations. The teacher gave a sidelong glance but returned his attention to the little old woman, who was giggling as her back grew progressively straighter.

"Peter addressed Bartholomew with some guttural instructions, and then shouted to the people pushing toward the teacher, 'Please, everyone, move back. The teacher will get to all of you, but you must make room for him. Stand back!'

"His words seemed to have little effect, and the disciples pushing back only compressed some of the people to where the

And He Healed Them All

most intense scuffle was happening. Someone swore loudly and people started falling over one another. I heard a loud crack from the bottom of the resulting pile.

"The old woman stood tall and graceful as she walked away, her hands raised and her eyes lifted to the sky. Two of the women with the teacher helped her through the tight crowd.

"The teacher waded into the struggling tangle of people, mostly men, where Peter and Bartholomew were trying to dig out whoever was on the bottom. As he pushed in, people backed away, making room for the teacher. This allowed Peter to make progress through the avalanche of arms and legs, and to work his way to the root of the pile.

"The teacher, meanwhile, healed a small man with a bandage on his head and helped him move out of the crush. The small man moved away with a laugh and a quick squeeze of the hand that the teacher held out to assist him.

"Finally, Peter stood over a man who lay on the ground grasping a large broken stick, what remained of his crutch. Peter picked up a shattered piece, about two feet long. The man reluctantly released the larger portion of the crutch when Peter pulled it from his grip to take custody of the potential weapon in a mob situation. The teacher took both pieces of the crutch from Peter. I expected the teacher to throw the pieces aside; as they had been doing with unneeded crutches.

"Instead, the teacher—also a master carpenter, remember—held the broken pieces up and pressed them together, joining them as they had been before the accident. As dozens of people looked on, the teacher restored the crutch to one single solid piece. He shook it above his head and bowed it slightly with two hands to show that it was restored. He handed it back to the crippled man, who still lay on the ground, propped up by one elbow. As he received his crutch, the man glanced between it and the teacher, no sign of gratitude for a healed crutch. Obviously the man had come for the healing of his lame leg.

"The teacher studied the man. I glanced at Peter and his other friends, who seemed to be the most perplexed. I overheard

Peter murmur, 'Okay, James, what is he doing now?'

'"Why would he bother to fix a crippled man's broken crutch?' Bartholomew said.

"The cripple searched the face of the teacher. He tipped his head to the side. The teacher smiled and nodded. He reached out his hands, taking the crutch in his left hand and grasping the lame man's outstretched hand with his right. The man leaped up, both feet firmly planting on the ground. He looked down at his legs, one of which had recovered even as he stood up. The formerly crippled man grabbed the crutch from the teacher's hand and stabbed it toward the sky, shouting triumphantly.

"Even the trampled and bruised people around him laughed and shouted along with the healed man. The release of the ensuing celebration loosened the tangle of people so that the men who had been pushing and cursing now helped one another off the ground.

"The teacher focused his attention on healing those who had been part of the pileup that broke the crutch. There didn't appear to be any serious injuries resulting from the incident, but he healed minor scrapes along with preexisting sicknesses, deafness, missing teeth, and even a man missing both of his thumbs.

"The teacher and his friends restored order and the crowd slackened their forward press. Into the space before the teacher stepped a man quite distinct from the majority of the crowd, a gaunt, tall, dark man in foreign-looking robes, a turban on his head. He bowed to the teacher, with an extra nod of his head. He did this without taking his eyes off the teacher. Behind the stranger stood four or five other men similarly, but less elaborately, dressed. One of these translated for the distinguished stranger.

"'I am a magician from Syria, where I have many followers and my power is well-known. However, in spite of my powers, I am unable to heal my own illness; neither can any of my disciples nor the other magicians from my area. I do not know what my ailment is, other than to say that I am weak and tired most of the time. I spend many days or even weeks in bed. Some days I am struck with a fever. Most days my appetite is nonexistent.'

And He Healed Them All

"The magician's face remained unmoved, stoic while he explained his problem and his disciple translated. Then he held out a bag of coins, which another of his disciples had passed to him. But the teacher raised his hand, palm forward.

"'What I have is given freely, not purchased.'

"The magician accepted this response and offered his double-jointed bow once again, as if in apology and deference.

"The teacher stepped toward the magician but looked past him to one of the foreigner's disciples. The teacher pushed up the man's headdress slightly. The young man was missing his left ear. Without hesitation, the teacher poked the scarred place where the ear had been. The young disciple, a man with nut-brown skin and black eyes, jumped back. I wasn't sure why he reacted that way. Was it the suddenness of the teacher's movement, the impropriety of bypassing the magician, or the healing power hitting the side of his head? Regardless, the disciple stumbled backward, but the crowd pressing behind him kept him from falling.

"While the crowd's attention had been briefly diverted to the stumbling disciple, the teacher turned back to the magician. He motioned for him to put his hands out in front of him. The teacher placed his hands on top of the upturned palms. Within a few seconds, the magician winced, as if his hands were unbearably hot. Yet he kept his hands there. Before a minute had passed like this, the magician collapsed to the ground, as if all of his joints had broken loose and nothing remained to hold him upright. It happened so fast, his followers were barely able to break his fall.

"The teacher moved on to touch the next person to his right as he followed the line of the crowd before him. Behind him, the magician remained on the ground, shivering and making a sort of stuttering noise. The mostly Jewish crowd maintained a suspicious distance from the foreigner."

Walter paused and reached for his water.

I smiled at him, speechless at first. Then I opted for practical considerations instead of the dozens of spiritual and emotional issues raised by the dream narrative.

"I'll get you a little device that you can use for dictating your dreams, so you can remember more of the story."

He nodded. "So you think there will be more?"

I shrugged slightly and offered a hesitant grin. "It seems to me like you're just getting started."

Walter shifted in the bed, sitting up straight, and reached for his favorite Bible. The energy with which he did this startled me, but I withheld comment, intimidated by where he might be taking this conversation. I hadn't read a Bible for a decade, at least.

"I've been trying to fit the dreams into the Gospels." He adjusted his glasses when he found the passage he wanted. "It says here in Matthew chapter fourteen verse fourteen, 'When Jesus landed and saw a large crowd, he had compassion on them and healed their sick.'" He looked up at me.

I didn't respond, still feeling out of my depth.

"There are a bunch of stories like this, Jesus healing a whole crowd of people, many more accounts than I was aware of before. I guess the preachers I've been listening to haven't gotten around to those stories yet." He raised both eyebrows.

Walter drew a deep breath, and I prepared for one of those lectures that had enthralled me as a student.

"I think it's too easy for us church people these days to just skim these words and not let them find traction in our souls. Think about this. This is not some holy automaton just doing what he was programmed to do. This is a living and loving human being who had feelings for those who were suffering. But how could it be any other way? He was Jesus, the living sign of all the love God has to offer. How could he look at the sick and the injured and not be moved?

"But, of course, he was not just teary-eyed about what he saw. He took care of them. Jesus's feelings were normal, as was his desire to respond. For him, healing them all was normal.

"I don't know about you, James, but the people I see these days doing healing on TV seem anything but normal." He chuckled.

I joined his laughter, but I was struggling with my own inconsistencies. The cinematic detail of these dreams seemed to me a serious challenge to the flaccid faith I had evolved. He seemed to sense my preoccupation with this internal guilt-fest.

"What are you thinking, young man?"

I smiled, not feeling so young as when he first called me that twenty-some years before. "I've strayed a long way from the faith my parents taught me," I said.

The steady gaze and warm smile that Walter beamed my way made me feel like he was proud of me for finally addressing that particular elephant in the room.

"I'm glad you're thinking about that. And I think there are more of these dreams to come, so you'll have plenty of time to keeping thinking about it."

Chapter Four
New Mercies

When I left Walter that Wednesday night, I drove directly to a store where I had seen a display of digital recorders designed for dictation. In part, I intended this to relieve Walter from having to remember so much detail, but I was also feeling an obligation to help him get these stories onto paper as soon as possible. Fulfilling my promise gave me the excuse to head back to Walter's place Friday evening.

I made arrangements over the phone for a wheelchair and planned to take him out to dinner as I did occasionally. This time would be special, however, because Jillian was going to join us. At this point in our relationship I was still dumbfounded that she was available to go out with us on a weekend, instead of weeding through a long queue of romantic options. Which is to say that I wasn't seeing her very objectively or thinking of her anymore as just Walter's psychiatrist.

Helping Walter to put on his coat and hat that evening in his room, I noticed that he had some limited use of his right hand. Looking back now, it was apparent by then that, against all expectations, he had improved. Why I didn't say something at the time probably had to do with my struggle to keep the story of Jesus and his healing at a safe distance, locked in the pages of the Bible. Then again, I wasn't used to the nursing functions that had intruded into our relationship, like getting Walter dressed, the nursing staff typically did that sort of thing.

In the midst of my awkward efforts, Walter provoked me with a teasing bit of news.

"I had the fourth dream last night."

I finished tugging his weaker arm into the sleeve of his tan and brown winter coat, testing a half-baked hypothesis that had occurred to me. "Is it possible that these keep coming because you want them to? Is this some sort of self-fulfilling prophecy?"

He waved his left hand as if shooing away a pesky fly. "When did you ever hear of someone controlling their own dreams? In fact, isn't that the point of a message delivered in a dream? It comes when we're off guard, when the subconscious mind has sway over the conscious."

I laughed in acknowledgement of my dubious question, revisiting my discomfort with the way Walter had so firmly concluded that these dreams were a divine message to him. If a stranger in another room of the convalescent home were reporting these dreams, I would have doubted their authenticity. But this was Walter, the most stable and trustworthy person I had ever known.

Jillian arrived in Walter's room just then, diverting the conversation and leaving me with a head full of questions, questions fired at me from some unseen attacker, or maybe just a playful friend.

The logistics of getting Walter into and out of my car added another reason I could be thankful for Jillian's presence. Walter's use of his one good leg helped, and he didn't weigh over a hundred fifty pounds by then, but that all didn't add up to easy and intuitive transitions.

It was nice to have a professional to consult when Walter halted my clumsy efforts with a bellowing plea. "Hey, you're gonna brain me while you're messing with my bum leg there." I could just barely detect the musical tone of a good-natured tease in this complaint, and that only because I knew that Walter had reverted to his playful and vocal self. A stranger might have taken him seriously and reported me for abusing the elderly.

"Sorry, about that Walter," I said.

Jillian stepped quickly to the other side of the car and

reached through to give Walter a hand to grasp in his effort to slide onto the seat. Meanwhile, I made sure to avoid knocking him unconscious. I knew we had done okay and he was in good spirits when he tried to talk Jillian into staying in the backseat with him. Trying to steal my date.

"Okay, old man. One miracle at a time, how about?"

We all laughed as we assumed our expected seats and got on our way to the restaurant.

Arriving at Walter's favorite steakhouse, I realized for the first time that I would have to cut his porterhouse for him and wondered if my caregiver skills were up to that challenge. After drinks and salads, I still harbored these concerns until Walter stopped the waitress who brought the steaks.

"Young lady," he said with a twinkling squint up at her. "How would you like to cut my steak for me? There'll be a big tip in it for you, I assure you." He gave me a wink. I was paying for dinner.

Finally, after the rich, salty meat and potatoes had been dispatched, we sat with half-eaten desserts and cups of hot coffee, while Walter told us part of the latest dream.

"The crowd continued to press toward the teacher, filling in after each person who received healing and then walking or running to wherever friends or family were waiting. I noticed one small boy getting pushed back repeatedly, being shoved aside as others tried to reach the healer. The slim boy with large dark eyes looked to be about nine years old. His skin seemed tanned by the sun, and his curly black hair was brown from the dust stirred by the crowd.

"When people gasped and cheered as the teacher restored sight to a blind man, the boy tried to push into the brief void the blind man and his son left, great smiles on their faces and tears on their cheeks. But an old man with a grotesque lump on his neck pushed through ahead of him. The teacher touched the lump without a word and it disappeared.

"When that man left, his hands raised to the sky, shouting praise, the little boy tried again, only to be cut off by a woman and the man with her. However, the teacher seemed to look right through that couple. He spoke directly to the little boy, even though I was sure the couple hid the boy from the teacher's view.

"'Little boy, come around here so I can see you.'

"The boy turned his head and looked to either side of him then back toward the teacher's voice. A tall man standing by the boy evidently understood. He tapped the shoulder of the woman ahead of him while guiding the boy forward.

"The teacher squatted before the boy so that they were eye-to-eye. 'What do you want me to do for you?'

"The boy hesitated, and just when I thought he was too shy to speak, he blurted, 'It's not me; it's my father.' The people around him exchanged looks and seemed to search for the boy's father.

"The teacher kept his eyes on the boy. 'Where is your father?'

"'He's at home in our village, over on the other side of the hill.'

"Murmuring arose from the people close enough to hear. They seemed either amused or indignant at the thought of the boy asking the teacher to go elsewhere.

"'You see all of these people, of course.' The teacher waved his hand to indicate the crowd. 'How would you have me help your father if he's not here?' The teacher's tone was not shaming or ridiculing, but instructive.

"The boy seemed undeterred. 'You could come there when you're done here.'

"'Possibly.' The teacher nodded. 'But I'm traveling in the opposite direction when we're done here.'

"The boy twisted his lips, a thoughtful look crossing his face briefly. 'Then maybe you could send one of your disciples.'

"'My friends are all needed here with me. Why didn't someone bring your father here to me?'

"'He can't walk, and he is too big for my mother and me to carry. No one in our village would agree to carry him this far. My father is a very big man.' I heard an edge of pride in the boy's voice, even though his father's size was causing a problem just then.

"The teacher patted the boy's thin shoulder. I had the feeling that this was a sort of exercise. The teacher didn't seem at all concerned that the alternatives the boy proposed proved impractical.

"The people around them, however, grew restless. They edged in tighter, and scowled at the young boy. Murmurs and grumbling increased. Clearly, the teacher chose to ignore them and remained focused on the boy.

"'I think you will have to do it,' the teacher said.

"'Me?' The boy pointed to his chest.

"'What is your name?

"'Noah.'

"'Hold out your hands, Noah.'

"The boy obeyed.

"The teacher reached toward the boy's slightly grubby hands. The moment their hands touched, Noah's face opened in surprise, eyes wide, lips moving wordlessly, and his whole head tipped back as if pushed by a strong wind.

"'What do you feel?' the teacher said.

"'It's . . . it's hot . . . it's alive . . . it's. . . I don't know what it is.'

"The teacher breathed a slight laugh and then put on a more serious face. 'Take that to your father. Put your hands on him when you enter your house, and he will get well.' The teacher stood.

"Noah stared up at him wide-eyed then looked down at his hands, which appeared to be vibrating, not like one would do voluntarily or like palsy, but faster and more precise, as if those little hands were charged with electricity. Noah didn't speak. He didn't even say thank you. He just looked at the teacher and then back at his hands.

"With his hands held up in front of him, like someone who couldn't find a towel on which to wipe after washing, he tried to turn and make his way through the crowd. He seemed fearful to touch anyone standing in his way. I imagine he didn't want to lose the power his hands held. The teacher must have seen the boy's dilemma, for he motioned to one of his friends. 'Andrew, help him get through.'

"Obedient, Andrew stepped in front of the boy and pushed gently through, excusing himself and asking people to step aside so the boy could go through unhindered. Andrew and Noah disappeared into the crowd.

"But I wanted to see what happened with him and his father. No sooner had I formed that thought than I was with the boy, watching him leave the edge of the crowd, as Andrew waved him on with a word of encouragement and a smile.

"Still, Noah held up his hands, but he stopped looking at them, so he could see where he stepped along the rocky way. His pace was halting and uneven with his hands raised like that. People stared at him as he passed, but he seemed not to be distracted by their curious glances. He was on a mission, and, like any nine-year-old boy with a clear goal in mind, he seemed focused only on completing that mission.

"Noah walked for nearly an hour with his hands held up, though I knew he must be growing weary of holding them that way. He held them out as if he were carrying a small log in front of him. His pace remained uneven but urgent.

"He came upon a woman sitting by the side of the road, a small boy lying limp in her lap. The woman was crying. Her long hair strayed from her head covering, her eyelids were swollen and red, and her cheeks seemed sunken with weariness. Noah stopped to look at the little boy. Then he looked at his hands again. They were still vibrating.

"Noah spoke softly, as if only to himself, 'The teacher said to put my hands on my father and he will get well.' He looked to the boy.

"He took a step to continue on his way, but the woman stopped him. 'What's wrong with your hands?' She sniffled. Even in her obvious grief, the boy's strange behavior seemed to puzzle her.

"'Nothing's wrong. I just saw the teacher who's healing people on the mountain over there.' He nodded back the way he had

And He Healed Them All

come. 'He touched my hands so I could go home and heal my father. He is very sick and too big for me and my mother to carry.'

"The woman sobbed. 'I was taking my little Joshua to see the teacher. But he seems to get weaker and weaker as I carry him along. And I am so tired. I don't think I can carry him another step. She pulled the end of her head covering over her face as she cried.

"Noah stood still. A variety of emotions crossed his face. I wondered what was going through his mind.

"'You should go on home; your mother is probably wondering where you are,' the woman said when she noticed Noah's hesitation. 'Do as the teacher told you.'

"Noah seemed physically pained to leave her and her sick boy. He looked back up the road he'd been traveling. 'Is your son going to die?'

"The woman could only shake her head and cry.

"Noah stepped over to the woman and her son. 'When the teacher touched my hands, I felt something happen to them, and it's still happening. I think when I touch my father he'll get well, like the teacher said. But I don't think the teacher would mind if I tried touching your little boy first to see if he could get well too.'

"'But what if the healing power leaves and you can't heal your father?' The mother sniffled and scowled.

"Before she could stop him, Noah reached out one hand and put it on the smaller boy's head. 'He feels really hot.' Noah's eyes grew round. 'He's getting hotter!' Noah quickly withdrew his hand from little Joshua's head. He looked worried, as if he'd hurt rather than helped the boy.

He jumped back, however, as the Joshua opened his eyes.

"Both Noah and the mother gasped. Joshua struggled to sit up in his mother's lap, nimble little arms and legs awakening in four directions at once. She let go of him to allow him to maneuver, and then she suddenly sat up straight. She shouted. 'His skin is cool. His fever is gone!' She hugged her squirming son, who was no longer flush from the fever.

"Noah looked at his hands.

And He Healed Them All

"'Have they stopped vibrating?'

"'I think so—Wait! The vibration is back, stronger!'

"Noah and the woman laughed.

"'Oh, thank you, you've made us so happy,' the mother said. 'You have saved us both. Thank you so much!'

"Noah turned to leave then stopped. 'I guess it was really the teacher who healed you. He put the healing in my hands.'

"The mother nodded and hugged her child again, watching as Noah turned and skipped toward his house.

"The little village in which he lived lay very quiet when Noah arrived less than a half hour later. The rugged and narrow lanes of the hamlet stood empty. The late morning sun radiated off the whitewashed walls and revealed the mud and manure stains where the walls were not so white. But Noah looked only at his hands and at the path.

"He passed a neighbor's house just when the door swung open and a little girl, about six years old, stepped out carrying a bucket. 'What's the matter with your hands?'

"Noah stopped. 'I'm doing something very important, Rachel.' A big boy's hubris fueled a harsh edge to his voice. Then Noah seemed to repent. 'Come and see.'

"Rachel didn't hesitate to follow Noah. In fact, she proved helpful when he stopped and looked hard at the door handle to his house. I could imagine that he questioned touching it with his vibrating hands. Rachel solved his conundrum by opening the door for him.

"'Thank you.'

The two entered the house.

'Mother?'

"No answer.

"The house was dark inside, the shutters closed on all sides. The sparsely furnished home contained the barest necessities. Noah walked past the table to his parent's bed against the far wall. A partition shielded most of the bed from view. Noah moved around it. He motioned with his head that Rachel should join him.

"The large man was still breathing, though his breath was raspy and uneven.

"Noah stood there. He seemed undecided as to what to do. But it wasn't long before he stepped to the edge of the bed, leaned over, and put his hand on his father's forehead, perhaps the way he had seen his mother touch him to check for fever.

"'I think he has a high fever, just like the little boy on the way home,' he said. Noah kept his hand in place for several seconds.

"'What are you doing?' Rachel said.

"'Waiting for something more to happen.'

"'What?'

"'I'm not sure.' He leaned closer to his father. 'Do you think he's breathing easier?'

"Rachel shrugged.

"Noah stepped back. He studied his hands; they no longer vibrated. He looked like he was about to cry.

"'Noah?' His mother said as she stepped through the opened front door.

"'What are you doing?' a girl about twelve said. I assumed she was his sister.

"Before Noah could answer, his father stirred. All eyes flew toward him. He propped himself by one arm.

"Noah's mother screamed a short note of surprise. His sister dropped the firewood she was carrying on her feet, but made no complaint about the pain.

"A huge smile stretched across Noah's face.

"'Well, what's going on here?' His father seemed baffled by speechless gathering.

"Rachel looked a bit perplexed. I figured she didn't understand what had taken place. But as six-year-olds are wont to do, she told on Noah. 'Noah was holding his hands funny, and then he told me to come and see, and he touched your head, and now you're sitting up and speaking.'

"Silence filled the small house as all eyes went to Noah. He quickly explained all that had happened with the teacher, his vibrating hands, the woman and her son on the side of the road, and then when he touched his father.

"Still stunned, his mother took Noah's hands in hers to examine them. Rachel pushed her way in to get a closer look, but Noah's father just laughed, sat up, and pulled his wife into an embrace.

"After the hugs and laughter dissipated, Noah's father asked his wife to bring water for him to bathe. 'I feel like I haven't had a good bath in a long time.'

"Noah's mother threw open all of the shutters, bringing in fresh air and sunshine.

"In a flash, I flew from Noah's house to return to the teacher, leaving behind a bubbling family that was attracting the attention of their neighbors, particularly because Rachel ran around telling everyone she could find what she had seen and heard.

"I hesitated in that miraculous flight to watch the woman whose boy Noah had touched by the road. She walked with her little boy next to her. He stepped spryly, asking one question after another, stopping now and then to look up to check his mother's reaction.

"Then back to the crowd on the mountain I flew.

"The teacher had moved from where he was when I left. Between where he now stood and where I had left him, dozens of people lay scattered on the ground. At first, I thought these were people whom he had not yet touched, who lay where they had been placed by friends and family. Then I noticed that none of these people lay on mats or stretchers. In fact, the area where the people on stretchers and mats had been laid earlier that morning was filled with people standing, trying to push closer to the teacher.

"As I arrived, a man with a very severely curved spine stood hunched in front of the teacher. The teacher placed a hand on the man's chest and then slapped him on the back rather forcefully. With that, the man straightened, let out a yelp, and promptly fell backward, laughing and praising God. The teacher smiled at the man now on the ground at his feet, but he quickly moved on to the next person.

"That's when I noticed that most of the people I had seen lying on the ground were smiling, crying softly, or laughing. This was the aftermath, not the lineup, of those needing to be healed."

Walter laughed and stopped there. For a moment he sat staring into the dim restaurant, grinning euphorically, completely oblivious to Jillian and me. At that point I realized something I had unconsciously detected. Walter seemed to reside more persistently within the dreams as he narrated them. He seemed to struggle more to return from the journey on which those dreams led him.

Finally, he turned and smiled at me self-consciously, glancing briefly at Jillian as well.

Jillian teased him. "Welcome back."

I laughed at her plucky freedom with Walter. The boyish fascination he showed toward these dreams made him more approachable than the venerable old professor I knew before they began.

A new waitress offered us refills on our coffee, though we had already paid our check and simply hadn't bothered to leave yet.

I sipped briefly from my cup as she poured Walter's. I noticed that he had managed to get his right hand up onto the table. I was thinking that I hadn't been paying attention to exactly what he could and couldn't do after the stroke. But Walter pulled my attention back to the dreams.

"Do you think Jesus would have really done that with the little boy, put healing in his hands?" he said.

Jillian set her cup in the saucer. "Sure, why not?" She adjusted herself in the heavy wood and leather chair, sitting up straighter. "If you read the Gospels, you see the disciples were sent out to do the same sort of healing Jesus did. Given the shortcomings those guys displayed throughout their time with Jesus, if God could use them in that way, then why not an innocent boy?"

This was the first time I saw clearly that I was outnumbered. A small part of me complained that I had fallen in among these true believers, but I ignored that minority report and nodded at Jillian's point. "Yeah, I remember some of the stories about those fishermen and tax collectors arguing over who was most important, or something."

Walter's voice sounded apologetic. "I guess I'm looking for some affirmation that these dreams are as real as they seem to me."

Jillian smiled a sort of motherly approval.

I responded. "I know they're real to you. I've seen you getting inside the story. To me that's proof of how real they are."

Walter's grin stretched into a yawn and I looked at Jillian.

"We'd better get you home," she said, reaching for Walter's scarf, which hung over the back of his wheelchair. With maternal tenderness Jillian wrapped the scarf around Walter's neck as he attended to the way it covered the front of his shirt. Then we both helped him with his coat.

We did all of that with a minimum of words, needing little to communicate among us. In that silence, I ran back over the dream and the longing it stirred in me. Longing for what, I couldn't say, but then that's the most tenacious kind of longing, isn't it? The kind we can't define or name.

In spite of our late night, helping Walter into the car didn't frustrate or scare any of us as much as the first time. Some of the improvement seemed to come from Walter discovering ways he could help, even with his weak arm and leg. I noticed Jillian studying Walter for a moment from the seat next to him before moving up front with me. When she returned to the front seat next to me I looked at her, hoping to figure out what she had been thinking, but she lowered her eyes and faced forward. She didn't return my attention.

I discovered what she was puzzling about when we arrived at the retirement home, and we assisted Walter back into his wheelchair.

Holding his right hand, the one that had been affected by the stroke, Jillian questioned him as he settled into his little metal chariot. "You do have some use of your right side now, don't you, Walter?"

As I finished guiding his right foot into the silver stirrup, he answered. "Yes, some use." He looked Jillian square in the eyes, craning his neck a bit to do so. He grinned a nearly symmetrical grin. For a moment I thought Jillian would say something, but she seemed to be almost holding her breath.

This interaction struck me only in retrospect. At the time I was full-speed-ahead into perfecting my elder-care skills and getting all of us in out of the cold. The accumulating fog from our breath was threatening to become a major weather system.

With Walter drowsily in the care of Roxanne, his favorite nurse, Jillian and I left him with warm thanks going both ways; Walter grateful for our taking him out, and both of us grateful for his telling of the latest dream.

On the ride back to her house, Jillian's breath came in smaller and smaller puffs of vapor as the car warmed up again.

"Are you working tomorrow?" I said, though I felt a little like I was breaking into her ruminations.

She snapped her head toward me, as if I had suddenly just arrived.

"Tomorrow?" She seemed to be trying to fit that word into something that made sense at the moment. "Oh, yes, I am working tomorrow. It's one of those Saturdays when I get together with families of the residents."

Not comfortable with interrupting someone's meditations, I let the conversation fall, curious about what was preoccupying her, but too nervous to ask. I suppose that simply revealed my lack of security in our relationship, as well as my lack of comfort with the implications of the dreams.

Jillian insisted I stay in the car and not walk her to the door. This created a dilemma for me, torn between old-fashioned chivalry and modern egalitarianism, but also feeling a bit put off by her. I don't know if she meant it that way, but I worried that she was keeping me at a distance.

Chapter Five
What's Going On Here?

The following Monday afternoon, I walked into Walter's room to find Jillian standing next to his bed, tugging at a pencil in his hand. This tug-of-war stopped me in my tracks. "Walter, did you steal Jillian's pencil?"

Jillian let go of the pencil. They both smiled at me like mischievous children.

Their goofy grins intrigued me. But I kept up the joke. "If not, then Jillian, you should know better than to steal pencils from defenseless old people."

Jillian stood up straight and gave Walter a sideways glance. She laughed.

Walter protested. "Who's defenseless?" He switched the pencil to his left hand and brandished it like a sword.

I looked at Jillian for a more serious response.

Still smiling, she said, "Walter seems to be recovering some motor skills he lost as a result of the stroke." She sounded every bit the physician but as giddy as doctor who'd been drinking on the job.

I guess I wore a puzzled look, both from trying to absorb her explanation and her uninhibited laughter, because when she turned her full attention to me, she sobered.

"James, Walter is being healed as he dreams of healing."

I stared into her clear, nimble eyes. My thoughts tripped over her words, only to stagger when I looked into her open and inviting face, so close to mine.

And He Healed Them All

Walter intervened. "James, let me tell you about another dream. Maybe it will do as much for you as they've been doing for me."

A fifth dream? I shook my head as the news siphoned my pool of untamed thoughts into a simple desire to hear the next installment.

"Tell me."

Jillian took my hand and led me to one of the chairs next to Walter's bed. We both sat down.

Walter slowly laid his pencil on the table next to his bed.

"When this next dream began, my attention was on a man standing in the crowd, watching. I say watching, because he was letting people go before him to get to the teacher, not pressing forward like everyone else. He seemed to be there simply to observe, yet genuinely curious and apparently much impressed by what the teacher was doing. As I watched, he wiped a tear from his eye at the healing of a feeble old woman receiving sight in an eye that had been blind for a generation. As she raised her hands to praise God, the watcher started to do the same and then pulled his arms back.

"'Joseph, come here.' The teacher broke into the watching man's anonymity.

"For a moment, the observer stared wide-eyed, evidently surprised by the teacher's request. The teacher motioned for him to come. Joseph pushed past several people and approached the teacher.

"'Joseph, what do you see?' He waved his hand toward those who'd received healing and were dancing and praising God.

"'Teacher, I see the hand of God at work. I see a day that my ancestors dreamed of for centuries.' His voice cracked and his eyes welled with tears.

"'You believe, then?'

"'Yes, Lord, I do believe.' Joseph held his chin high as he declared his heart. He seemed to stand taller as he put his faith into words.

"The teacher nodded. 'Good. Go back to your home country

for now. In two years, come back to Jerusalem, where you will find something new, and you will take part in what God is doing in the world.'

"Joseph furrowed his brow, as though not understanding what the teacher was talking about. Regardless, he bowed slightly to the teacher and stepped back.

"The teacher stopped him. 'What about your stomach?'

"Joseph raised his eyebrows and brought his hand to his stomach. I thought I saw him wince.

"The teacher touched Joseph on his midsection before he could reply. After a one-second pause, Joseph doubled over as if in severe pain. The teacher helped him slowly collapse to the ground.

"He said, 'Your stomach pain will be healed, but you will have a fire in your belly that will not go away. Pay attention to that fire, Joseph, and you will know what to do.' The teacher left Joseph sitting on the ground, holding his stomach like a woman in labor.

"As the teacher moved back to where he had stood before, several boys moved quickly through the crowd. People parted to let them through. Three boys were carrying a fourth, who was bleeding from a wound near his collarbone. The wound was clumsily wrapped, and the cloths were soaked red.

"The teacher met them, kneeling as the boys lowered their friend to the ground. He spoke to the others in a soft voice as he put his hands on the wounded boy's chest. 'What happened to him?'

"The tallest of the three looked at the other two. 'It was the Romans. They shot him with an arrow.'

"'Why did they do that?'

"Again the spokesman used his eyes to check with his two companions. 'We were throwing rocks at them.'

"When he said this, the teacher removed his hand from their friend's chest. People near enough to hear what was going on murmured things like, 'What did you expect?' and 'Serves them right.'

"The three friends exchanged looks out of the corners of their eyes, while keeping their heads down. They certainly heard the murmuring around them, even if it had not occurred to them that their crime, or at least their foolishness, disqualified their friend from the teacher's help. But when they turned back to the wounded boy, they found his eyes wide open. He said, 'How did I get here?'

"The three helpers frantically assisted the wounded boy when he tried to stand, and the adults crowding around vented their astonishment that, in spite of the blood-stained shirt, the boy appeared perfectly healthy. The teacher smiled at the four boys as they embraced one another, searched for the missing wound, and breathed relieved sighs interspersed with jokes and teasing. They quieted when they caught the teacher eyeing them, one brow cocked, and his arms crossed over his chest.

"'What will you do when the Romans pass your way the next time?' he said.

"The three boys who had carried their wounded friend exchanged glances again while clearly frozen into guilty stiffness. But the wounded boy, whose hand was still clasped to his formerly pierced chest, smirked. 'Throw bigger rocks?'

"The teacher laughed and shook his head as the other three pushed and goaded their resurrected friend. The teacher tousled the hair of the boy he had healed. 'Live long, my boys. Act wisely, and survive to see your grandchildren.'

"They thanked him and bowed. As they moved to leave, the teacher touched the arm of the boy who had been shot. The teacher was holding out his hand. The boy reached up. The head of a Roman arrow dropped into his hand, still coated with blood. His smile disappeared and he looked up at the teacher with wide eyes, as if reality had landed in his hand and penetrated his heart.

"As the four boys pushed back through the crowd, the teacher asked Phillip for a rag to wipe the blood from his hands.

"By this time, a caravan of people from Samaria had reached the front of the crowd, the whisperings of many disgruntled Jews revealed their origins. These people dressed similarly to the local Jews, but with a more Roman or Greek style to the way they wore

And He Healed Them All

their hair or their sandals and head coverings. As I've learned from my research, they looked like Jews in exile. But they were Samaritans, considered quite separate from the Jews, both by the Jews and themselves.

"The first of the Samaritans to receive the teacher's attention was a stout young man who said he was a blacksmith by trade. He unwound a bandage from his left hand, which had been severely burned and was nearly black with infection. The man gingerly held his hand out to the teacher. But the teacher's response was not delicate; he grabbed that hand as in a handshake. The young man opened his mouth as if to scream in pain. Instead, he looked down at his hand as the teacher held it. The burn, which had included the back of his hand, would have been visible had it still been there. The blacksmith's open mouth stayed that way, his eyes wide. Just like so many others, he came for healing yet seemed shocked when the teacher actually did it. The teacher released his hand and the blacksmith stared at it as if he had never seen it before.

"Turning to Matthew, the teacher asked for some water to drink. Instantly a dozen people produced goat skins or gourds containing water they had brought for their journey. The teacher took a water skin from a boy about twelve or thirteen years old. He thanked him, took a long drink, and then, instead of simply returning it to the boy, he poured some of the water over the boy's head. The boy shrugged his shoulders tightly against the sudden shock of the water, and then he grabbed at his lower back. He shouted, 'It's healed! My back is healed.' As he instinctively spun to look to his healed back numerous droplets of water flung in all directions from his wet hair, sparkling beads flying in the bright sunlight. As the droplets splashed on people nearby, each person, at least six, simultaneously began to shout and demonstrate how their bodies were no longer sick or in pain, moving arms and legs, necks and backs. In all directions little swirls of activity resulted from each revelation of healing.

"The teacher turned his attention to a woman standing with a teenage boy. 'My son cannot speak,' she said, raising her voice against the boisterous celebration of the newest cluster of miracles.

"The teacher addressed the boy. 'Look at me. Open your mouth.' He carefully touched the boy's tongue and removed his finger quickly.

"The boy's mouth clamped shut; then he opened his mouth and made some sounds. He didn't seem to be trying to form words; rather, he seemed thoroughly fascinated with his new ability to make inarticulate noises. His mother thrilled with the significance of those meaningless sounds, laughing and rejoicing like a mother whose life had just been transformed

"The teacher moved on, nodding in response to the mother's thanks. He faced a man and woman with a little girl, whom, the man held. Without hesitation the teacher took the girl in his arms. The man, who I assumed was her father, released her without a word. The little girl, about four years old, stared wide-eyed at the teacher as they met face-to-face.

"'What do you want?' he asked the girl.

"'I want to sleep all night without coughing. I'm very tired, and Mommy says I should sleep so I can get bigger.' Her skeletal arms and legs, her bulging eyes ringed with shadows, and her ragged hair testified to her body's inability to thrive.

"'Okay, then you will sleep all through the night, without any coughing, from now on.'

"The girl raised her eyebrows and pursed her lips. 'Are you coming to my house tonight?'

"'No, I won't be coming to your house this night. Do you live far?'

"Her father answered for her. 'Only a few miles, sir.'

"'Well, then,' the teacher said, looking to the little girl, 'you will go home tonight, and as soon as you finish your bedtime prayers, you will know for sure right in here'—he pointed to her little chest—'that you will have no more coughing problems.'

"'Is God going to take my coughing away?'

"'Yes, God is going to take it away.' He handed her back to her father, both parents thanking him, as he stroked the girl's back one more time before moving on.

"Matthew and Philip propped up an old woman as the teacher approached. She had to turn her head sideways to look up at him out of the corner of her eye because of the harsh curve to her spine. Her hands lay folded on the top of a cane. All of her fingers showed the swollen twist of severe arthritis.

"'Do you want to be well, Mother?' the teacher said.

"'Why, yes, of course.' Her voice sounded like a rusty hinge.

"The teacher rested his hand on her shoulder, and she jolted, as if being electrocuted. The jolt echoed up through the arms of the two men who had been supporting her. They managed to remain standing, holding the woman between them. Her head rolled from side to side and then settled in the middle, her eyes closed. Her cane lay at her feet now, her hands in front of her, shaking.

"Again the teacher touched her, and again she trembled so that Matthew and Philip shook as well. She stood up straighter each time the teacher touched her. Her eyes still closed, she seemed to be concentrating on something. Her lips moved but no sound emerged.

"A third time the teacher touched her. This time she raised her hands, falling over backward and making a sort of singing noise as she slowly settled toward the ground in the arms of Matthew and Philip. A woman who was with the teacher's followers stepped through the men and covered the old woman with a blanket. She knelt next to her to guard her from the crush of sandaled feet.

"The teacher touched the hands of a young woman who then grabbed her abdomen and smiled. He turned to his left and touched the forehead of a man with bandages on his ear and neck, and then back to his right he touched a woman propped up by a pair of men, one older and one younger. The speed of his movements translated into a frenzy of bandage removal, crutches tossed aside, and hands waving in worship and praise. Several people now danced near the teacher, including the little old woman he had healed of severe arthritis.

And He Healed Them All

"The music and movement of worship captured my attention. But a young woman standing perfectly still off to one side also caught my eye. She stared, oblivious to her surroundings except for one person. Her eyes never left the face of the teacher. She seemed completely smitten and her eyes followed his every movement. Then I noticed another person, a man with a face lined with years, mesmerized by the teacher. He held his knotty hands up, palm to palm, in front of his mouth, completely absent from the world around him except for the teacher. Then my view broadened and I saw that dozens of quiet worshippers stood all around. Like the singers and the dancers, they also worshipped the God who had sent the teacher. These silent, heartsick admirers had recognized the one truly loving person and could not tear their eyes from him.

"Mary, one of his followers, directed the teacher's attention to a couple holding a very tiny baby, sheltering the little one from the noise and bustle around them. Mary and the teacher approached the couple. My focus moved in close with them. The little girl barely breathed and made not a movement. Mary and the teacher completed the shelter for the little one as praise and dancing continued among the well and the sick alike. Only a few people near the couple and their little baby seemed to sense the drama unfolding in the miniature shelter of the four adults hovering over that small life.

"The teacher cupped one hand entirely over the little face and head. When he popped his hand away, the baby gave a tiny little cough. She stretched all four limbs and opened her eyes. Her marble eyes rolled from mother to father and back, her lips curled into a smile. The teacher smiled too. Mary clasped her hands against her cheeks and watched the beautiful little life, admiring the baby's every movement and expression. The teacher patted Mary's back and stepped away to assess the activity around him."

Walter took a deep breath.

"I think that's enough, for now," Walter said, implying that more of that dream remained to be told. He sat still, staring vaguely ahead as he usually did when he ran out of momentum for telling about a dream.

I noticed the digital recorder on the night stand to his left.

"Did you record this one?" I asked, nodding toward the little silver device.

Slowly bobbing his head for a few seconds, Walter found his voice again.

"Yes, I recorded it in the morning after I woke up yesterday."

"A Sunday dream," I said.

His smile turned impish, his eyes squinting so that the fan of lines deepened on both cheeks. "Yes, instead of going to church to meet with Jesus, he comes to me in my dreams."

I laughed just briefly, recalling Jillian's assertion that the healing had moved out of the dreams and into Walter's body. I looked at her. "Walter's improvement . . . is that what you were trying so hard to figure out Friday night?"

Jillian smiled, raised one eyebrow slightly, and gently shook her head as she studied her own hands for a moment.

"I guess I'm a little ashamed of myself," she said, looking first at Walter and then back at me. "It was obvious at the restaurant, and especially after he told the dream, but I just couldn't spread my imagination far enough to allow the truth inside." She raised her face slightly and stared down her angular nose at me. "I guess I was having one of those 'too good to be true' moments."

I recognized the quote from our first dinner together. I also thought I recognized a look in her eyes that included me both in her confession and her revelation. But I decided to release that string, at least for the time, and turn my attention back to Walter. "How long have you known?"

He squinted then raised both bushy gray eyebrows. "I wondered about the added sensation in my hands after the first dream. Then I found that I could move my fingers and toes slightly after the second one, and so on."

"So it's been going on this whole time, but gradually?" I said.

"Yes. And I'm with you two on this. I just couldn't believe it was for real, even though I was experiencing it myself. That's why I waited to be sure before I said anything." He blinked and lowered his eyebrows. "But I'm realizing that wasn't a good plan; 'cause if you want to doubt, you'll just keep on doubting, even as the evidence piles up."

"'Want to doubt?'" I said.

He swept us both into his gaze and into his confession. "I think we have to admit that doubt is as much a choice as faith is."

I knew he was looking inward and including himself in this declaration, but that statement couldn't have hit harder if it had been a hatchet aimed at my chest. I realized in that moment that I had not only chosen doubt, but I had nurtured it and multiplied it over the years until church lost its meaning, the Scriptures grew dusty, and my heart had room for only me.

The past days of revelation and introspection piled up on that brief comment like a crash in bumper-to-bumper traffic. I took a shaky breath that drew both Walter's and Jillian's attention. Jillian reached out a hand and held my arm, but none of us knew what to say. They seemed as daunted by the unfamiliar territory as I was.

Chapter Six
What It Takes to Believe

I visited Walter again on Wednesday that week. To my surprise, he had eaten his dinner while sitting in his favorite chair, fully dressed in a maroon cardigan sweater, a button-down-collar shirt, and slacks. From head to toe he looked a hundred percent better than any time during the past year. His face seemed to deny his age and certainly retained no signs of the debilitating stroke he had suffered so recently.

"Well, now you're just showing off." I teased him.

His wide grin showed some teeth. He looked relaxed with his hands resting on the arms of the soft velvet-like chair, his cardigan contrasting nicely with the pale blue fabric.

He chuckled. "Oh, you know me too well. I really did want to flaunt my newfound strength, though we'll have to save the arm wrestling for later."

I laughed and scanned the room for a place to sit. The bed looked like my best option, with the good chair taken and a pile of books in a smaller, less comfortable chair on the other side of the room. As I climbed onto his bed I asked about the books.

"Looks like you've been doing some reading."

"Oh, yes. The Internet is a wonderful thing, at least when it comes to finding resources."

"Looks like you have enough to keep you busy for a while. Just let me know when you're done with those, and I'll visit the college library for you, if you want."

"Thank you. I may take you up on that."

I propped myself comfortably in his old spot. "On the phone you said you wanted to tell me the rest of that last dream."

"Oh, you want to hear about that, do you?"

"Yes, professor," I said like an obedient child.

Walter smiled and began. "The teacher continued to push into the crowd. Celebrating their healings, or that of family or friends, people had begun to slacken the push toward him, fragmenting the mass of humanity that covered the hill. There were, of course, still many hundreds of people waiting to be healed.

"Through all of this, a young boy carrying a lamb approached. A large, round woman at the edge of the crowd asked him, 'What are you doing here with that animal?'

"'I want to see the teacher,' the boy said.

"'See him about what? He's quite busy healing people, you know.'

"The boy avoided answering directly. 'I want to see the teacher,' he said again. He ducked behind a group that was edging closer to the teacher. The woman shook her head as he disappeared from her view.

"The teacher was helping a woman to stand. As he held her hand, her legs shook and it looked like some concealed person was lifting her up off the ground. And then she stood on her own legs. Her robe was now too short for her fully developed limbs, and more than one woman put her hand over her mouth at the exposure of so much skin. But the healed woman seemed not to notice, for she walked a bit, turned, then spun and jumped. She danced for the joy of it. As she danced with arms and legs each following a different rhythm, I realized that the miracle of her healing also included being able to walk without the sort of physical therapy typically required after any kind of repair to muscle or bones.

"The boy with the lamb took advantage of the attention drawn by the dancing woman to slip through several clusters of people, nearly reaching the teacher. The boy was, in fact, close enough that when a man grabbed him to hold him back, the teacher saw the confrontation. 'Hey, where do you think you're

And He Healed Them All

going?' the man said.

"'I need to see the teacher.' The boy squirmed in the man's grasp.

"The teacher intervened before the conflict escalated. 'Bring him to me.'

"Philip urged a couple of people aside to make a path for the boy. He gestured for him to approach the teacher. The boy glanced at the teacher and then followed Philip's gesture, still mindful to lean to one side to avoid the man who had tried to stop him.

"'What do you want, young man?' the teacher said.

"'My ewe lamb is crippled. She can't keep up with the herd, and she even has a hard time feeding from her mother.' He set the lamb on the ground to demonstrate. The lamb tottered, falling to her left.

"Peter voiced a protest. 'Teacher, all of these people are waiting, and this is only a scrawny little lamb.'"

"But the teacher put up his hand, even as a small chorus of indignant voices percolated around them. The teacher swept his gaze across the complainers, who grew quiet. He picked up the lamb and scratched her behind her ears. She nuzzled his hand. Then he simply set her back down and ruffled the hair of her young shepherd before moving on to the next person.

"The little lamb stood with all four legs firmly planted, no sign of weakness. She gave a skip and made a move to bolt, so that the boy lunged to keep her from escaping. Several people laughed or exclaimed when they saw the little lamb healed. The boy shouted, 'She's all better now. She can walk! Oh, thank you, master, thank you.' His tanned little face bloomed in a big, crooked-toothed smile, even as he struggled to get control of the spunky, gray lamb.

"The teacher acknowledged the boy with a smile, even as he held his hand on the forehead of a man with a skin disease. The man was kneeling before the teacher in a position of prayer, his hands clasped in front of him, his eyes closed, and his head raised toward the teacher. Along the left side of his face ran a dark red rash. For one second his whole face turned red enough to match the rash. When the flush faded, the rash faded with it. The thin, middle-aged man opened his eyes wide as his hand explored where the rash had been. He yelled a grateful exclamation and stood up, throwing his arms around the teacher's neck.

"Immediately, James and Peter stepped up to pry the man's hands off of the teacher. They did this so automatically that it occurred to me that they certainly had seen how this kind of thing could get out of hand. How tired the teacher would get from healing so many in one day, especially if he had to embrace every one of them.

"The teacher smiled at the man and clasped his hand, even as his two protectors pulled the grateful worshipper away from him.

"An older man approached with a young woman, perhaps his daughter, leading him by the hand. It seemed that his sightless eyes had left him totally dependent. The teacher touched the man, who threw his head back and shouted, momentarily frozen in that position.

"The teacher stepped to a little girl held by a man who may have been her father, her face bright red, her eyes watery and glassy. The teacher blew in her face with breath that seemed to contain the exact color the little girl's face *should* have been. Now pink and fresh, she leaned her head on her father's shoulder and smiled.

"By this time, the blind man stood still, a confused look on his face. 'What is it, father?' his daughter said.

"'There is light, much more light than I have seen for a long time, but it's all one color, or a swirl of colors, like water moving.'

"'Oh.' Her voice dropped with apparent disappointment. 'Maybe we should try again. Maybe he would touch you again.'

"'Yes, of course. He's not finished; he just needs to finish.'

"The teacher had ministered to several other people since touching the blind man; so the man and his daughter had to work their way through the crowd again, the father still needing her help to lead the way.

"The teacher saw them approaching and turned to meet

And He Healed Them All

them. His relaxed smile and bright eyes seemed to say that he knew exactly why they approached a second time. Again, he received the blind man. This time with both hands he gently touched the man's closed eyes. Then he was off to heal others, leaving the man exclaiming at what he saw, as he nearly pitched over backward. His daughter laughed at him. He covered his eyes with his hands, and then moved his hands slowly away.

"'I can see my hands, but they don't seem clear to me. They're blurry when I hold them away.'

"Evidently the man's eyesight had improved markedly, but it was still not perfect. The healing was not yet complete.

"Once more father and daughter wove their way through the crowd. Less in need of her help, he nevertheless hung on to her. The teacher stopped his progress to reach back and touch the man once more. The teacher didn't even bother waiting for them to meet him face-to-face; instead, he reached over the shoulder of a man he had just healed of deafness and touched the not-so-blind man. The old man stopped stone still, his eyes fixed firmly on the teacher. The teacher lingered, allowing the man's new sight to focus on him. The older man's satisfied silence testified to the finality of his healing.

"Then the teacher was on the move again, pausing to take some bread handed to him by Peter, followed by a quick drink of wine. While he was still chewing and swallowing, he faced a woman and two teenage girls. He wiped off a few crumbs, brushing his hands down the front of his robe. The two girls, probably in their late teens, stood on either side of the woman, who was about twice their age. She said, 'Teacher, my name is Hannah, and these are my daughters.'

"The teacher attended to her words and glanced at the girls.

"'They have been living with their aunt—my husband's sister—in Jerusalem, for two years. That woman has given herself to the power of evil spirits so she can do divination and spiritual healing.' Her tone escalated. 'And she taught this to my daughters, exposing them to the power of these spirits.'

"This information helped explain some odd behavior I had

observed between the two girls. They didn't look at each other, but their faces moved slightly, in the way that one does in a conversation. They appeared to be communicating with each other without words. This annoyed the teacher, it seemed, for he ordered, 'Stop that.'

"The command seemed to startle the two girls, who acted as if the teacher had caught them misbehaving. They looked at each other briefly and then lowered their eyes, avoiding the teacher's.

"The teacher addressed them. 'Do you want to be free of these spirits? Do you choose to let go of this power?'

"They checked with each other. 'Yes,' they said simultaneously.

"The teacher nodded. But when he reached for their hands, both girls stepped back.

"Their mother grabbed their arms. 'You have to let him do what you're asking him to do. Do you want to be free or not?'

"The teacher shot the mother a sharp look. She released her hold and the girls returned to their places directly in front of the teacher under their own power.

"Each girl let him take a hand. I had the impression that they had just attached themselves to a power source that was not entirely pleasant to touch. They had duplicate reactions. At the first touch, they stiffened and vibrated. Then they appeared to almost rise, as if blown by a wind coming from the teacher. Each girl clung to the teacher's hand with one of her own, but the other limbs blew in that strange wind, such that they never seemed to have more than one foot on the ground at a time.

"The teacher almost bellowed. 'Do you want to be free of these spirits? Do you choose to let go of this power?'

"It seemed that neither girl could speak, but they both managed to nod their heads haltingly against the force that radiated from the teacher.

"At their recommitment to deliverance, the teacher said, 'Go!' And that word seemed sufficient to sever the girls from their illicit spiritual connection to each other, because immediately they both relaxed and landed with both feet on the ground, one hand still held by the teacher, the other hand loose by their sides, heads bowed, hair curtained over their faces. Only then did their separation manifest, as the girl to his left fell backward to the ground, and the other tipped forward. The teacher caught her and held her there for a second while she regained her equilibrium. The girl he held straightened, brushed her hair from her face then looked at her mother. The two lunged for each other and embraced then stooped to help the other daughter, who had collapsed into the arms of strangers standing behind her. She untwisted her gown and joined the smiling embrace of her mother and sister.

"Stepping aside to leave the three women to their reconciliation, the teacher reached for a boy of about ten years with a crutch wedged under one arm. The boy looked up at him, locking on the smiling face of the teacher, even as he took away his crutch. The boy didn't try to stop him; instead, he immediately stepped down on his injured ankle. His countenance brightened further as he put more and more of his weight on that foot, until he stood only on the formerly injured foot, his face like someone who is finally getting a joke at which everyone else is already laughing.

"The teacher gave him a friendly pat and stepped past the boy to an older woman lying on a mat carried by four young women.

"'This is our mother,' the one nearest to the teacher said.

"The mother's complexion was as pale as her linen sheets.

"He leaned down and whispered, but not into the woman's ear, rather into her mouth, as if breathing the words into her. The woman did not move as the teacher stood and looked around at the girls. They all drooped even as they stood, strands of hair escaping head coverings, hands strained to red and white as they clung to their corners of the stretcher. Again, he leaned over the motionless woman and spoke softly as before. This time her mouth moved in response. All four girls gasped at this sign of hope. As her color visibly brightened, they began to weep. Within a few seconds, her eyes fluttered open. She looked at the teacher as if she knew him. The teacher and the mother didn't exchange any words, as if everything had already been said. She surveyed her girls. Her clear and steady eyes seemed to reassure them that they need fear no longer. Her smile wiped away their drooping weariness, but nothing could stop their tears. The teacher and his guards moved on as the four girls lowered the stretcher and helped their mother stand, watching her steadily regain strength.

"Focused now on a man with a heavily bandaged hand, the teacher took hold of it as if it were healthy. The injured man pulled back at first, his instincts evidently still in charge. But then he stopped, seemed to assess his hand, raised his eyes to the teacher, and then pulled at the bandage.

"One of the teacher's followers offered to help the man as the teacher moved to the next person. Perhaps embarrassed by his dirty bandage, the man refused help, choosing rather to rip at it with his teeth.

"The teacher stood before a man who cradled a little boy. The boy's head and neck were swollen and red, such that he scarcely looked human. The teacher touched the boy's taut skin with his fingertips. 'Go away.' He spoke with a quiet resolve.

"The boy stirred, coughed, and blinked open his eyes; his color changed and the swelling lessened. By the time the teacher had moved to address the next person, the boy was already scrambling out of his father's arms, looking curiously at the people around him. He held on to his father's robe with one hand and inched away, following the teacher with his dark eyes.

"A man with bandaged knees and using crutches hobbled into the teacher's notice. His movements jerky and sporadic, he moved like a man whose long journey, and the long wait in the sun, had worn him out. His eyes, however, showed clear and expectant as the teacher approached.

"'You are healed,' the teacher said, moving on to the next person. While the teacher touched and healed a little girl with a red and swollen ear, the man with bad knees walked in a small circle, loosely holding a crutch in each hand.

"Just as the little girl received her complete healing, the man with the newly restored knees shouted, 'Thank you!' He tried hopping a bit, kicking each foot in turn. He looked around, locating the clearing where abandoned crutches and stretchers had formed a small mound. He headed that way, flinging his crutches onto the pile then beginning to remove his bandages.

"Beyond the little girl with the inflamed ear, the teacher beckoned for a gaunt man in ragged clothes to step forward. He looked to be in his fifties, and was as thin as I could imagine a living person being.

"'What would you have me do for you?' the teacher said.

"'My stomach is bad, I can't handle food most of the time, and I can eat only certain things,' the emaciated man said.

"The teacher touched the man's stomach. From the thin man's reaction, you would have thought the teacher had punched him, because he doubled over, moaning. He dropped to his knees.

"The next man mirrored the first one's ragged testimony to a life of poverty. When the teacher approached him, he became agitated, his hands and feet beginning to churn, looking like he was trying to find an exit. When the teacher grabbed a flailing hand, instantly the man calmed. He appeared to be suddenly fixated on the teacher; all of his frantic motion and vigilance disappeared. He stared through renegade strands of dirty hair.

"'Shalom,' the teacher said.

"While the teacher remained focused on the second man, the first one stood up from the ground. He smiled the relaxed smile of a man thoroughly at peace. He looked at Peter, who stood behind the teacher. 'You wouldn't happen to have any food about you?'

"Peter located one of the teacher's other followers, and pointed to the thin man. 'Joanna, this man needs something to eat, more than anyone I've ever seen. What can we give him?'

"Joanna smiled and reached into a basket of bread. She pulled out a round loaf and offered it to the hungry man. He accepted it with enthusiastic thanks.

"Watching that man eat captured the full attention of many of the surrounding people. His gratitude for his simple meal was so apparent that it infected many who witnessed his recovery. The pleasure of watching him enjoy that bread inspired several others to offer him more food and wine. He didn't refuse anyone until his arms were too full to take more.

"Joanna and Peter led him to an open place and laid out a blanket for the man to sit on and eat a decent meal away from the sympathetic gazes of so many people. The two helpers yielded only briefly to the temptation to watch him enjoying his food so thoroughly. As Peter turned to leave, the man said, 'Maybe you could join me; it seems so strange eating all this alone.'

"Peter chuckled and looked around. 'There's probably someone here who can use this more than I can.'

"The teacher had finished with the second ragged man, who seemed lost in a private cloud of satisfaction. Peter grabbed the opportunity to bring him over to join his friend. Both men could obviously use a meal.

"The teacher had moved on to a group of young people, teenage boys and girls. They clustered around a boy, about fourteen, who leaned on two of them for support. He appeared to have several physical difficulties. Not only were his legs misshapen so that he couldn't stand on his own, but his eyes were sunken into his head, likely entirely useless. His taciturn manner seemed to indicate a limited mental capacity as well.

"The teacher addressed the group. 'Who have you brought to me?'

"'Abner,' several of them said.

"'Abner appears to have many friends.'

"One girl stepped forward. 'Everyone loves Abner. He's never harmed anyone. And so many things are very hard for him. We've grown up with him in our village, not far from here, and we were all hoping that you could do something to help him.'

"The teacher nodded. 'Yes, I *could* do something for him.' He smiled slightly, as if joking with the young people. He stepped close to Abner and took hold of his hands. The teacher looked into Abner's hollow eyes for half a minute without saying or doing anything else. Then Abner seemed to jump a bit, but I think this impression came actually from his legs suddenly straightening.

"Abner laughed. He tipped his head down and began walking in place, trying out his new legs. A cheer rose from his friends, and Abner joined the cheer, with his hands raised over his head. But clearly the teacher was not finished. He helped Abner to step back a bit, then bent down and spat in the dust where Abner had been standing. With one finger the teacher stirred the spit into the dirt to make a small patch of mud, and then he scraped the mud up off the ground with the back of his thumbnail.

"The teenagers stared with wide incredulous eyes and open mouths as the teacher carefully rubbed the mud on Abner's sunken eyelids. As strange as it was to see the teacher rubbing mud on the boy's eyelids, it was stranger still to see those eye lids begin to swell. Then Abner blinked a few times before fully opening his eyes. With his new eyes wide open, he made a sort of crowing noise and fell over backward. His friends caught him and kept him on his feet. They cheered at the restoration of Abner's sight. Though still upright, he reeled in a circular motion such that I expected him to fall in any given direction. But his feet began to pump up and down, as if he were running in place on legs powered by an engine.

"The teenagers cheered again. All of them, including Abner, jumped up and down with their hands raised above their heads. Their shouting turned to singing, their song a dancing praise from an ancient psalmist. For a moment I thought that the teacher would join their dance, but he made only one stomp on the ground and then dropped his hands to his side and moved on to the next person who needed him."

Walter finished there.

Of course, I had never seen Walter drunk, but if I had, I imagine he would have smiled at me just like he did then, unconsciously shaking his head in micro motions. I was curious how what he had seen had made him so high.

"Did you cheer along with them?" I wasn't teasing.

Walter shook his head, his grinning gaze falling far beyond me. He chuckled, and then it bloomed into a full-throated laugh.

He laughed so hard that tears came to his eyes.

I watched and wondered, beginning to feel a bit disoriented myself. I couldn't focus a clear thought, reduced to shaking my head in those same tiny sideways motions, and to wiping a tear out of the corner of my own eye.

Finally, Walter wiped at the tears with both hands, swallowed, and took a deep breath. He looked around for his water glass, which I reached for him so he wouldn't have to turn so far around.

After a gulp, he returned the glass to the table. "James, this is like nothing I've ever even imagined. You can see why this is so real to me. How could I create these scenes in my head? I've never experienced anything remotely like this." He stopped to catch his breath.

My perception of all this came one very large step removed from what Walter saw in those dreams. But I knew Walter. I had sat in his house and waited while he cried uncontrollably at his wife's death. I had also sat there cursing about the end of my marriage. I could count on Walter like the predictable and inevitable changing of the seasons and the setting and rising of the sun. And here I sat watching him either slip hysterically into insanity or rise euphorically into a spiritual experience for which neither of us was prepared. I couldn't see the dreams, but I could see what they were doing to my old friend, and I envied him more intensely than anyone I've ever known.

At home that night, I couldn't sleep. My belly seethed with conflicted emotions that I couldn't name but which started with my realization in Walter's room that I knew the dreams were true. They were true in the sense that he was entering the experience of Jesus healing an entire multitude of people, and true in that the Jesus in the dreams was a real person who accepted and cared for every person who brought him their pain and weakness. And he powerfully liberated and healed every one of them.

This revelation convulsed my stomach because it collapsed my world, my construct of reality. I thought I had risen above the primitive faith of my childhood and conquered the world with systems of rational thought that all pointed to humanity's self-sufficiency, my self-sufficiency. But all of that glorious enlightenment turned sour, and even rancid, if Jesus was real and alive and speaking to Walter through those dreams. In fact, he was speaking to *me*, wasn't he?

I thought of my wasted efforts to build a life with God as merely a convenient background, even a handy punching bag for my intellectual self-promotion. And my sleepless downward spiral continued. When I hit bottom, or what seemed like the bottom at that late hour, the backlash started.

What was I going to do about this anyway? It was easy for Walter; he had retired and was looking at the end of his life. So close to heaven, he had little to risk from becoming a religious fanatic. Me, I had a career to consider. The ethics classes I taught allowed for objective consideration of religious, even spiritual, claims. But that was God at a distance, or more accurately *gods* at a distance. What was I supposed to do, renounce all I had taught over the last twenty years?

This sent me in search of what I had said over the years about people of faith, religious true believers. I wondered whether I had gone too far and cursed myself in the process. At this point, I realized that I hadn't even gotten close to the bottom yet. I had just found a brief pause on a narrow ledge, off of which I dropped still deeper as soon as I moved.

Such were my feverish thoughts as I finally fell asleep, in spite of the science experiments someone seemed to be conducting in my gut. My last conscious thought was that I should talk to Walter about all this . . . and maybe Jillian too.

Chapter Seven
A Friend in Need

The next two days I called and talked with Walter only briefly, planning to see him Saturday afternoon again. I phoned Jillian too and invited her over to cook supper with me. Pretty comfortable in the kitchen, I thought it would be a safe place for us to talk about my crisis of faith, or lack of faith, perhaps.

Friday evening, Jillian appeared at my front door for the first time. I could tell that she had taken time to go home and change. She looked comfortable in a long gray cardigan and jeans, her hair down from her proper psychiatrist style. The cold outside had only done her a favor, turning her nose and cheeks slightly pink, to resemble a little girl by the fire at Christmas. Such were my distractions from more important matters, including supper and the state of my soul.

"Hello, how are you doing?" I kissed her briefly on her chilled cheek before taking her coat from her.

She breathed a purging sigh. "I'm doing quite fine. Glad to do something with my hands that doesn't involve a life-or-death situation." Though she had a playful smile in her blue eyes, it was the closest thing to a complaint I had heard from her—not much, considering it was the end of the work week.

"What about you?" she said.

I led her to the kitchen. "I'm glad for the weekend. Too bad you're tired, though, I was hoping for a free therapy session after dinner."

She smiled, her eyes narrowing just slightly as she checked to be sure that I was kidding. "As long as it doesn't involve confessing any major crimes, I think we could arrange that."

I laughed. "Yeah, I guess then you'd have to contact the authorities and that would really ruin dessert."

"We're making dessert too?" She scanned my big old kitchen, rubbing her hand along the butcher-block countertop on the island that stood in the center of the dark stone tile floor.

"Actually, I already made it. Just homemade chocolate pudding. It's chilling in the fridge."

"Homemade chocolate pudding!" The corners of her mouth stretched toward her ears.

"You like chocolate, right?"

"Yes, indeed. You sure got that right."

As it turned out, Jillian was the perfect kitchen assistant. I think the end of a long work week helped. She was glad to let me give directions and was perfectly content to do whatever needed to be done. Together we made a variation on a meal my mother used to make. Homemade noodles with beef and mashed potatoes.

When I explained my plan, she scowled. "You trying to fatten me up or something?"

I grinned at her across the butcher block. "Oh, you don't have to eat it. You just have to help me cook it." We laughed together.

We drank wine and chopped vegetables for salad, rolled out the noodle dough, and boiled water, not talking about anything more serious than childhood memories of our mothers in the kitchen and foods they cooked. The fun rolled by quickly, as did the warm and savory meal. I thought I could see Jillian's face loosen and heard her voice slacken as she relaxed in my house. It was a great thing to see. I really missed knowing a woman who felt at home with me.

While we cleared the table of dishes, Jillian surprised me.

"So what is it you wanted to talk to me about?"

"Wow," I said, settling plates in the sink and rinsing them absentmindedly. "You took me seriously, huh?"

"You're a pretty serious person," she said, as she put the salad dressing back where she had found it in the fridge. "Even when you joke."

I was thinking I should be paying for insight this sharp. "Yeah, I gave my agenda away, I guess. I really did just want to spend time with you, though." I looked up from the dishes and met her eyes as she stopped next to the sink. Her smile had given way to an open and peaceful face, her comfort with me clear in how close she stood and how steadily she looked at me. I knew she was waiting for my answer. I was just enjoying watching her wait, but not enough to leave her in suspense.

As we put dishes in the dishwasher, made coffee and broke out the pudding, I replayed my thoughts after my last visit with Walter. She asked only brief, simple questions, though I could tell she was listening the whole time. Her eyes rarely left mine, as she let me keep my hands busy, my unbroken succession of little tasks reducing her to the role of spectator. It reminded me of watching my mother work her magic in the kitchen, though she usually didn't seem as nervous as I was that night.

Everyone should have a skilled psychiatrist over for dinner once in a while. For the price of some noodles and chocolate pudding, I got top-notch care. I finished my rant at about the same time she first dipped into her pudding, a tiny dab of whipped cream included on that first bite. She let the silence remain between us as she enjoyed a couple of more bites of dessert.

"This is wonderful," she said. "I don't remember the last time I had this." Her grin was contagious. "You know what my favorite part is?"

"Not the skin on the top." I took a sip of creamy coffee.

"Yes!"

"I think it used to gross me out when I was a kid. Guess I grew out of that," I said.

She nodded. Then she returned to my flush of anxiety that had preceded dessert. "It goes against our training, I know, but a bigger perspective of the way the world works has to include the power of a spiritual experience or revelation." She took another spoonful of pudding. "We're trained to put together systems, to believe only in things that we can reproduce in a laboratory or a syllogism. But life confined to that level isn't really satisfying to anyone I've ever met. We all need something more, mystery, romance, an encounter with the divine, probably all of that." She laid down her spoon and picked up her coffee in her two lean hands.

I sighed and stopped eating. "That's what I want. I just need the courage to break out of my tidy life and open up to the overture from God that Walter's dreams certainly represent."

"Yeah," she said after a few seconds. "It'll be easier if you don't have to try it on your own."

I looked at her and didn't say what I was thinking. "I know I need to engage more with Walter and the dreams. I know he's there for me." My voice felt drained, lacking the piercing punch of my earlier rant.

Jillian reached across the table and took my hand. "Not just Walter."

That, of course, was what I wanted to hear, the question I had avoided asking. All I could do in response was smile and look from her hand on mine to her eyes watching me in the dim evening light of my old house.

Before she left that night we agreed to meet in Walter's room the next day. Knowing I would see her the next day stifled my urge to try to keep her there as long as I could that night. We parted with a long hug and a warm kiss. I stood in the driveway with my hands jammed into my jeans pockets and my breath sending clouds after her parting car.

***

Saturday at the retirement home was as busy as usual, but Jillian was free to ignore the people crowding the hallways, or at least to try to ignore them. It wasn't obvious to all of the residents, or their family members, that she was there on her own time, so she had to stop and talk with a short, middle-aged woman with streaked white and black hair who needed reassurance about her father's mental condition. I waited behind Jillian, hoping the woman would get the idea that the doctor was on her day off. But I guess that wasn't clear, and Jillian answered the woman's questions thoroughly, and with the perfect focus of a portrait painter. I seemed to be the only one resenting the intrusion.

When we finally made it to Walter's room, he was sitting up reading, holding a hard-bound book with both hands. He looked up at us over his glasses, perched halfway down his nose, and grinned a greeting.

We each gave him the best hug we could manage while he remained sitting, though he did make a move as if to try to stand up. We discouraged the attempt, as least for the time.

I pulled a chair around for Jillian to sit in. "What are you reading?"

"A New Testament scholar writing about the ministry of Jesus, of course."

Jillian refused the chair, nimbly hopping onto Walter's bed instead. I stared at that girlish stunt and missed what Walter said next.

Walter followed my attention and craned his neck to see Jillian settling onto his neatly made bed.

"Oh, I hope you don't mind," she said when she noticed our attention.

Walter laughed. "No, of course not. Make yourselves comfortable. I have a dream to tell you about."

"Does it have a prominent religious figure in it?" I said.

"It does." He looked at me over his glasses, straight-faced.

"Go ahead," Jillian and I said almost simultaneously.

Walter jumped right in, only hesitating slightly for our childish laugher to die down.

"The sun hovered high in the sky by this time; and not a cloud marred the deep blue expanse. Near the teacher stood a girl about fifteen years old. I first saw her from her right side, her beautiful, dark, china-doll profile and a hint of her long shining hair. From that perspective her appearance was striking. But when she turned to face the teacher, I had a whole new perspective. Like a cruel joke, the left side of her face mocked the beauty of the right. Her muscles and skin hung loosely from her skull so that her mouth and jawline lacked shape.

"Her eyes sought the teacher under lowered brows and darted away as quickly as she met his scrutiny. Looking into her eyes, I knew that she was the saddest person I have ever seen. How many times in her life had someone seen her as I had, first from the right side, where she was so strikingly beautiful, and then they saw that other side, that other face, that other experience of who she was? How many smiles had she seen turned to shock or, worse, to derision?

"In her beaten and broken demeanor I thought I detected the depth of pain that her condition had inflicted. That too was more than skin deep.

"The teacher released the hand of a tiny old woman who had been paralyzed but now stood firmly on two feet. He smiled as she danced a little jig and raised her hands high. As she did so, he had to dodge to avoid a finger in his eye. Nudging the happy old woman gently so she would follow those who had been healed already, he moved to where the sad, young woman waited.

"He looked at her, or maybe looked into her would better describe it. Nearly a half a minute passed before the teacher spoke. She tried to return his gaze during this silence but couldn't sustain it for more than a few seconds. She kept trying, and then looking away, and trying again. Finally, she dropped her head and wept openly.

"The teacher put his hand on her shoulder. 'What is your name, little sister?'

"She shook with sobs, but I could just hear her mumble, 'Sarah.'

"He spoke to her like a man correcting a misunderstanding. 'This Sarah will not be barren.' His prophetic declaration seemed to break what resistance remained. She dropped to the ground, dissolving into more sobs and tears.

"The teacher knelt in front of her.

"'Sarah.' He spoke her name as if it were a spell or incantation, as if the very sound of it had power when it came from his mouth. She didn't stop weeping, but she raised her eyes to his. The teacher returned her look of longing, giving no hint of hesitation at the intensity of her emotions. The teacher spoke gently to her, like a husband consoling his bride or a loving father attending his mourning child. I couldn't hear his words, giving me the impression that even in my dream their conversation was too intimate for anyone else's ears.

"With all this, it occurred to me that the teacher had neither said nor done anything regarding her misshapen face. I even started to think that perhaps he might not heal her face at all. Wouldn't that be better, to teach her to love herself just the way she is? But this notion only shows the extent to which I was still myself in this dream, viewing Sarah with my own understanding and lack of faith. It was as if I hadn't learned a thing from all that I had seen in these dreams.

"Several people around them wept, some on their knees, apparently caught in the spirit of the intimate healing experience, even though many of them were still waiting for their own healing.

"Ministering so many people, the teacher often moved quickly from one person to the next. When he did pause, he often seemed to connect instantly with the person standing before him. But this time, it was like he launched himself into the very core of one soul. For whatever reason, he chose to linger with this young woman, maybe to savor the process of her healing, or allowing her to savor all of the healing that he had for her.

"Once more, Sarah looked at him, her sobbing somewhat abated. He reached up and held the deformed side of her face. At that moment, she seemed to enter a state of ecstasy, closing her eyes, tears streaming into her broad smile. I suspect that no one had ever ventured to touch that gruesome part of her. Within seconds, the teacher had massaged the distorted clay of her face into the shape God had intended. When he removed his hand, her face was symmetrical, her beauty complete. It was like a glorious work of art restored before our eyes.

"Sarah touched her face, stroking her cheek and tracing the line of her mouth, her chin, and her jaw. But still she looked at the teacher. He was her mirror, it seemed. The teacher stood; Sarah followed. In her gratitude she clasped her hands around his neck and hugged him.

"A look from the teacher stopped his friend John from intervening. With his own gentle hands, the teacher coaxed Sarah's hands from his neck. He spoke one last word, his eyes locked on hers. 'You are free now.'

"Sarah's eyes followed the teacher as he moved to the next person. She stood rocking slightly, quite wet with tears and, even so, she was the most beautiful woman in the crowd. She slowly turned and pressed her way through the gathered cornucopia of people, all of whom paused to look at her when she walked past.

"The teacher gently punched John in the shoulder when he noticed the younger man staring after Sarah. The two men exchanged a knowing glance and laughed. John bowed his head a moment, shaking it, still smiling. No doubt the teacher could read his thoughts, but this time anyone who saw the way he looked at Sarah knew what John was thinking.

"Two young men waited for the teacher to turn his attention on them. The manner of the connection between these two men seemed obvious to me, although I don't know if it was by some physical sign or some special knowledge given me in this dream. I simply knew that they had a homosexual relationship. I figured if I knew it, the teacher also knew. The way the two looked at the teacher, with mixed expectation and apprehension, eyes refusing to land on his face, repeatedly glancing away and at each other, suggested that they feared the possibility that he might condemn them for the deadly secret they shared. Surely, they both knew stories of men who were stoned to death for such a relationship, and they knew that many rabbis authorized such punishment. But what about *this* rabbi?

"'What is it you want?' the teacher said.

"I'm not sure whether he asked people this because he had no revelation about the nature of their ailment, or if some of them would benefit from openly expressing their need.

"The shorter of the two men spoke. 'I have this lump on my throat that is growing bigger and making it very difficult to speak or even breathe.' He pulled back his robe and raised his bearded chin to reveal a bulbous lump protruding from the side of his throat.

"The teacher gently touched the lump. Instantly, it disappeared. In that instant, the young man jerked back an inch and then took a deep breath. And he smiled. He began to praise God for his healing, his voice rising clear and strong. He grasped the teacher's hand and thanked him.

"When the teacher shifted to the next person, the two men hung there a moment, as if wanting to ask a question. The teacher appeared to ignore their sustained attention.

"As they remained, the teacher healed the swollen leg of a man who reeked of alcohol. Then he healed the uncontrollable tremors of a woman who wore the clothing of a prostitute. As the two young men witnessed this, I wondered if they saw a message for them in the way the teacher healed everyone and condemned no one.

"As the two young men turned to exit the crowd, the teacher touched a little girl whose back was bent as if she were an old woman. When he touched her, she began to shiver and shake then slowly stood up straight, as if invisible pulleys raised her head. She stretched a full foot taller than she had been only a moment before. Her eyes and mouth opened in wonder."

Walter stopped there. "There was more. I recorded it yesterday. This was just the part I remember most clearly."

He surveyed me for a moment, without words, then cleared his throat in a way that again called to mind when he used to teach classes.

Glancing briefly at Jillian, Walter explained. "I stopped where I did in telling you the dream because I didn't want to get too far from the girl with the misshapen face. I'm sure I didn't do that scene justice, but for me it was thoroughly captivating. I got so focused on the intensity of his eyes peering into her soul and her obvious vulnerability in his presence. Yet it wasn't the sort of vulnerability that leads to regret, if you know what I mean. I lost track of where I was for a while. The sun, the grass, the stones, the crowd seemed to fade way and I could only see the teacher loving her, and conveying that love before she was healed and made so beautiful." He lifted both hands to his chin, his elbows resting on the arms of the chair. "That's why he waited to heal her after he showed her with his eyes that he loved her, I think. He wanted her to know that he loved her no matter what, that she didn't need a perfect face."

He grinned at us, leaning on his right arm and looking at Jillian. "It reminds me of when I was a young boy and in love with Connie Tenopir." His attention ventured toward the wall behind me, as if his mind leaped into childhood memories. "I don't mean the story, I mean the feeling. It made me feel like a boy in love all over again." He chuckled.

He gestured to the book that lay on his nightstand. "I don't get any of that sort of feeling from these scholarly books, of course." He shook his head, closing his eyes briefly. "Jesus is this far-off historical character, part of this epic timeline of events, either religious or political, or both. He's not the gentle lover of a girl who hates herself for the life she's been cursed with."

Jillian nodded, her lips a straight line as she eyed the book.

Walter's scratchy baritone voice slowed with the weight of his thoughts and perhaps weariness from speaking for so long. "This is why we get the idea that we can just nod our heads at words about God and feel like that's enough. If Jesus is just an idea, or an ancient person way back there, then our hearts don't get locked in to something that stirs us and changes our lives." He looked at me then, as if waiting for me to say something.

Without planning where I was going I responded to the opening. "That's me. That's me all the way." I felt my breath rushing, shallow and rapid. "You must know it Walter. I've never cursed God or denied anything about him explicitly, but I just let

God get away. I let Jesus become that faded historical figure. It was like neglect instead of open rebellion."

Walter nodded, like he understood what I meant.

I felt like I had cracked open my soul like an eggshell.

"I think I figured out why these dreams came to me," Walter said.

Jillian and I spoke in unison. "Why?"

He snickered, but his eyes remained locked on me, his eyebrows lowered, lending intensity to his words. "After my stroke, when I was lying in this bed, unable to do much at all, I decided I had better check in with God. I started praying quite a lot in those first days. As I did, I realized how worried I was about you."

"Me? Why were you worried about me?"

"You seemed so unhappy, or at least so thoroughly not happy. I thought that you had allowed the weight of the losses in your life to crush your hope, your light. I hadn't really assessed it before, but I began to realize that you had faded away from your faith, and that lapse seemed connected with your bleak outlook on life."

I was speechless. He was right, so I made no effort to defend myself or resist his assessment.

"So I started to pray for you, to pray that you would find that spark again, that God would connect with you again."

I felt beads of sweat forming on my forehead, and yet my hands were icy.

"I think God gave us, not just me, these dreams in answer to those prayers. I know the dreams have literally saved my life, but I think they were primarily meant to save yours, James."

Walter and I had navigated some treacherous waters in our years of friendship, sharing our grief, our fears, and our pain. But Walter had never before spoken so pointedly to the state of my soul, never reached so deep inside of me and wrenched my heart free from its well-maintained display case in there. I tried not to break down crying, releasing the storm I had been containing in that floor model of my heart. Jillian slipped off the bed and knelt beside me, wrapping one arm around me and leaning her face on

And He Healed Them All

my shoulder.

For a brief window in time I returned to that Sunday school class with Sandy Schaefer's telling of what happened before Jesus fed the five thousand, how he healed all the sicknesses and injuries of the crowd gathered there. I flashed forward from that musty class room to Walter's disinfected nursing home room and the extraordinary coincidence of his dreams illuminating that *same* story. How unlikely.

I knew that Walter was not the sort of manipulative person who would have manufactured the dreams to match my childhood experience, even if he had known about that enigmatic Sunday school lesson beforehand. But apparently God observed no such restrictions against devious manipulations.

My two sensitive friends reclined their hearts it seemed, to allow me to silently spiral down into my own shocked thoughts, fully aware, I guess, that the one who created the dreams in answer to Walter's prayers would take care of their impact on my soul.

Chapter Eight
Finding My Way Home

I went to church on Sunday, for the first time since several Christmases before, and that previous visit was only to please my mother. This time Jillian accompanied me. Actually, it's more accurate to say that I accompanied her. And she didn't have to drag me there, not even metaphorically. With my expired faith, I had lost connections with any particular church. I had indexed the shortcomings of any congregation or minister I had associated with in the past, and that's not conducive to a warm homecoming.

Besides, I was falling in love with Jillian, so I fully expected to love whatever church she called home. I wasn't disappointed.

Instead of with cynicism and criticism, I greeted the songs and the preaching with the images of Jesus from Walter's dream. That view of God, and God's work through Jesus, rescued the church experience from the disappointments and distractions of the past.

After the singing and the sermon, and after I had survived re-introduction to the civil society of saints, we left the warehouse that the congregation had converted into offices, classrooms, and worship space, and we walked to my car. Jillian hooked her arm through mine as we made our way past friendly faces and half a dozen introductions.

"Pretty hospitable people," I said when we were alone.

"Actually, I think they're holding back." She glanced around and smiled. "I got a couple of waves from friends who normally would have talked to me. I think they were being careful not to scare you away." She laughed.

But I knew she wasn't joking. Her laughter, full of voice and girlishly awkward, sounded like relief.

"You've brought men to church before?"

"Oh, no, it's not that. It's just that my church friends are so overly invested in me finding someone, that they're on their best behavior this morning. I hope you know how many people must be praying for us just now." And again she laughed.

I marveled silently at this rare giddiness from the woman I had begun to know. I was glad to see the girl inside of her as she suppressed laughter and rolled her eyes at her own lack of inhibition. All I could do was laugh along. I could certainly relate to both relief and exhilaration with all I had experienced that morning.

After lunch I took Jillian home to fulfill her aspirations for a restful Sunday afternoon, though she did mention laundry, which never seemed completely restful to me. From Jillian's townhouse on the edge of town I headed back toward campus and the retirement home.

Walter greeted me when I found him sitting in the game room, soaking in the afternoon sun, a finished chess match on the board at his elbow. He looked thoughtful, as he did when he was working out a problem in his head.

"Looks like a victory." I noted the chess match. I draped my coat on the back of the chair opposite Walter and then settled into it.

He nodded slightly, apparently uninterested in talking chess. "It's good to see you."

I noticed the absence of a wheelchair. A walker stood between Walter and the window, a significant improvement over four wheels. "How are you feeling?"

"Getting better every day." A playful grin returned to his face. "The physical therapist saw me using the walker and talked about getting me into his torture chamber. I had to apologize for laughing at him."

I snickered and shook my head. "You're gettin' cocky."

"I think it's allowed. I'm not cocky about myself or anything. I know who's taking care of me. I get to visit him in my dreams."

I felt a stirring of jealousy at Walter's unique opportunity. He bypassed my hesitation.

"Let me tell you some more from that dream that I already started telling you about."

I laced my fingers over my crossed leg. "Please do."

"Back on that hill, though no longer near the top, for the teacher had been making his way slightly downhill, he stood among the scrub brush and sandy-colored stones. But what I saw most clearly was the people. He was working his way through pain and sickness and meeting the eyes, hands, and hearts of hundreds and hundreds of people.

"At this point in the dream, I remember three women standing before the teacher. They wore long cloaks in spite of the warmth cast by the sun. Those cloaks were not for warmth, however, but a clumsy disguise. For below the hem of those cloaks I could see that these three were not dressed like the rest of the women in that crowd. There was no rough cloth, often-repaired sandals, or hand-me-downs for these three. They wore gold-trimmed sandals, ankle bracelets dangling gems, and silken dresses that peeked out from beneath those cloaks. They were not just a little better off than the average people in the crowd; they were surely from some very fine house or even a royal court.

"'What can I do for you, ladies?' the teacher said, addressing them with a tone that made me think of when I met the mayor of my hometown, a well-known stately woman; certainly a different tone than his playful banter with children or his familiar respect for the elderly. I didn't sense that he was pandering to these young women; rather, I think he spoke in their language, with a manner they could understand.

"Then I saw that the two outer girls—for they were really teenage girls—supported the middle one. Her smooth young cheeks flushed as she responded. She bowed slightly, and then pointed to her ankle. 'I hurt my ankle, and it's not healing. It's too painful to walk on, and I certainly cannot—' then she stopped, as if remembering something she didn't want to let him know.

"He didn't wait for her to finish her thought. 'The doctors in Herod's court could give you no relief?'

"Her mouth gaped in surprise. I expect she was thinking the same thing as me: How had he known she was from Herod's court and not his brother's court or some other king's or prince's palace?

"Her friend came to her aid. 'She went to them and they couldn't take away the pain. They said to wait and it would heal, but it's been weeks.' She lowered her voice. 'If she doesn't get well soon, she won't be able to dance, and Herod will send her away, or maybe something worse.'

"I don't know what she meant by that, but the fiery glint of her eyes as these words pressed through her clinched teeth imparted a sense of danger.

"The injured girl spoke again. 'I know that I haven't been good, that I haven't been pure and righteous in everything. I know I've not been pleasing God, but I don't know where else to turn for help.'

"The teacher knelt down before her. 'How righteous would you have to be to deserve God's healing? How good would you have to be before you wouldn't have to apologize for asking for God's help?'

"The three girls stared down at him with their mouths slightly open. They looked like three carefully carved dolls, whose maker was in a strange mood the day he made them, so beautifully perfect and yet looking so confounded by what they were seeing and hearing.

"The teacher put one hand on each side of her ankle. She had firm thin legs, tapering to what had once been a petite ankle. The injured ankle was now gray, green, and blue, and swollen larger than her knee, which I could just glimpse as she lifted her leg slightly. Modest women who could see this covered their mouths, perhaps afraid that the teacher would be corrupted by such beauty, or maybe afraid that their own shame at being a woman would

And He Healed Them All

be exposed like that one thin dancer's leg. The teacher didn't act shy; he didn't hesitate to touch people, even the delicate ankle of a harem dancer. He even seemed unconcerned that he might hurt the swollen ankle.

"I saw the reverent stillness with which the girl received the touch of this holy man. And she spoke. 'Why do you touch me? Surely you know what life is like in that pagan palace. You know what things I am obligated to do there.'

"The teacher made no response.

"To my surprise, the dancer began to laugh. 'Oh,' she said as if suddenly out of breath. She tottered as laughter took over, and laughed until she could make no more sound. Evidently, she no longer felt pain, for when the teacher released her ankle, gone was the swelling and discoloration, and the girl was able to fully stand on it.

"Immediately he stood and addressed the girl on her left. 'And what about you?'

"She stared wide-eyed. Shaking her head, she took half a step back. 'But I have no injury; my feet and legs feel fine. I—'

"'Not that, of course, but the other thing that you dare not ask.'

"All color drained from her face. She turned to her two friends. The one whose ankle had been healed nudged her, still recovering from her laughter. 'Go ahead. Tell him. He'll heal you so you won't be thrown out of the palace, or killed.' She pressed her hand on her friend's back, pushing her forward.

"The teacher looked at the girl he'd just healed. 'Put your hand near the place.' She seemed to check with her friend first and then gingerly reached inside her friend's cloak below the golden sash. The ailing girl stood statue still and staring, her eyes wide.

"The teacher said, 'Don't be afraid. No one will know your secret. And soon there will be no secret for them to know.' He gently placed his hand on her shoulder and the first girl exclaimed and jerked her hand away. She examined her fingertips as if she expected some mark from a cut or burn.

And He Healed Them All

Her friend grabbed her own stomach. 'Oh! I felt that. I feel it. Something's happening. I know it's well. I am well!'

"She appeared startled. She had just been there to help her friend. Her large dark eyes, framed carefully in makeup, turned liquid with tears.

"She uttered a breathless, 'Thank you.'

"I couldn't help but think that her life was changed in that moment. Even if she went back to the palace, even if she danced before the king and his guests, and if she took part in the drunken orgies that followed, she would still know what it was like to be genuinely and purely loved.

"All three dancers thanked the teacher before they wove their way back into the crowd to return to their royal lives, but they didn't get far before encountering a circle of women who had been healed and were dancing in celebration. At first, the three girls stood by watching and smiling. Then a woman, about thirty years old, extended a hand to the girl nearest her.

"This was, of course, not the kind of dancing the girls did in Herod's palace, but they had been young girls once; they had surely danced at weddings, at bar mitzvahs, and births. They couldn't, however, dance in their cloaks. I suppose they scandalized many in the crowd when they cast them aside. But, for a few moments, they danced like little girls, for sheer joy and celebration.

"My attention went back to the teacher, who was holding a boy's wrist, watching a smile spread across his young face. Next to the boy stood a young woman who appeared to be far along in a pregnancy. Finishing with the boy, the teacher turned to her.

"She held one hand on her stomach; strain tightened the muscles of her face. A man stood behind her, holding her shoulders. His face wore the same tight look.

"'What's wrong?' the teacher said.

"'The child has not moved for ten days now,' the woman said.

"The teacher looked from her stomach to her face and to the man with her, who must have been her husband. The teacher rested one hand on the mother's stomach, next to her hand. He paused for a few seconds. 'What will you name him?'

"The couple stared at him, silent, as if unable to breath; he stared at the swollen belly as though seeing the hidden child. The man gathered his wits. 'Zebulon. We would name the child Zebulon if it was a boy.'

"The teacher nodded once, but he seemed preoccupied. The parents exchanged concerned looks.

"To their surprise, he spoke directly to the baby, 'Zebulon, wake up!'

"Immediately, both the teacher's and the mother's hands moved. 'Oh, my!' she said.

"The teacher smiled broadly.

"When the teacher removed his hand, the father ventured to put his hand there. Right away, his eyes brightened, clearly feeling the movement of his child. He smiled and sighed, a picture of relief. He lost that smile, however, in the next moment.

"The mother moaned and grimaced. 'Oh, my.' But this time her voice carried alarm instead of relief. 'I feel something.'

"'This is your first child?'

"'Yes.' Alarm rose in her voice.

"'Well, Zebulon is awake and it's time for him to be born.'

"The parents stared at him. The father spoke. 'You're saying he is to be born . . . now?'

"The teacher turned to one of his friends who stood to his left. 'Find a midwife, Thaddeus—now.'

"Thaddeus's eyes were as large those of the parents. He said nothing, but launched into the crowd. His voice cracked as he called out, 'Is there a midwife here? Is anyone a midwife?'

"The teacher motioned for the parents to follow Thaddeus. 'Go with him. Everything will be fine.' Then he caught the father's arm. 'You must raise this boy to be a leader among his people. He will be headstrong, but God will use that to the advantage of His purpose.'

"The baby's father nodded. He managed to say, 'Thank you,' before he followed his wife into the crowd in Thaddeus's wake.

"Already I could hear two women responding to Thaddeus's

calls and giving instructions to other people to do one thing or another.

"The teacher let the commotion pass before turning to a plump little woman who opened her mouth to speak, but the teacher preempted her.

"'Aren't you a midwife?'

"'Why, yes.' She sounded surprised.

"'Then you should go with them; they will need your help.'

"She nodded and turned to obey, but paused to reach quickly for her left ear. 'Oh, listen. I can hear now!' She faced the teacher. 'My ear is healed!' she said, as if he too should be surprised. He smiled and nodded.

"The woman laughed and began telling everyone she passed what had happened, even as she pushed her way toward the place that was being prepared for Zebulon's birth."

Walter stopped there. He hesitated a moment.

Waiting politely for him to finish his transition from the dream, I looked out of the broad windows to my right at a cold, but bright and sunny, day. I didn't want to interrupt that transition, as if fearing some ill effect— like waking a sleep walker.

After a moment, his focus landed back in the room, a thin smile on his lips, which appeared dry. "How was church this morning?"

I had told him of my plans to join Jillian that morning. "Better than I had hoped. I see why Jillian attends there, as do quite a few other counselors and social workers. Her church seems to have the kind of emotional sensitivity and honesty that she demonstrates every day."

"How does it feel to give up a Sunday morning?"

I smiled. "Oh, that's not much of a loss, especially compared with reconnecting with God and doing that alongside Jillian."

"I've been thinking lately. I wonder what church would be like if people could see what Jesus did firsthand, like I'm seeing."

From his restful, blue eyes and slight smile, I knew he wasn't taking a shot at churches, but asking an honest question. I knew his underlying concern had to do with the gap between the Jesus he was seeing healing all those people, even reviving the dead, and the Jesus folded and pressed into our churches. But I felt disqualified just then to say anything against anybody else's view of Jesus. I was still dealing with the great extent to which my own faith needed resuscitating.

Walter studied me and then faced the window when I didn't venture an answer. "Maybe you and Jillian will get a chance to see what such a church would be like, starting with the two of you."

My mind rushed to questions in four directions at once, none of which I felt easy about pursuing. Why just me and Jillian, and not Walter too? Did he expect the dreams to affect Jillian and me in some particular way? Could Jillian and I actually have an impact on her church, or any church? Did Walter have some foreknowledge about my future with Jillian?

I think he could see my wheels spinning. He settled my frenetic internal inquisition.

"All in due time, my friend, all in due time. You've really just started down this path."

I knew he was right about that.

Chapter Nine
Tipping over the Edge

The next morning, while I sat in my office scrutinizing a freshman ethics paper, Walter called me.

"Hello, James. I had to call you. I had another dream last night. I just finished recording all I could on that little gizmo you gave me."

I leaned back in my chair, happy to get some distance from that awkward and incomprehensible paper in front of me. "Does it feel like this is gonna go on forever?"

"Actually, this dream seemed to open the prospect of an end in sight, a hint that He can't keep this up forever."

Before I could ask what he meant by that a knock at my door interrupted that trip back into the world of Walter's dreams. The department secretary brought me a message and a late paper from one of my students. I also needed to prepare for my next class, so I had to say good-bye and wait to hear more of Walter's dream, an extremely unsatisfying start to my day. In fact, by late afternoon I couldn't take it any longer and skipped a department meeting to visit Walter.

I called Jillian to tell her I was on my way over. By the time I'd arrive, she was already in Walter's room, standing next to him. He sat near the window and the heating vent. He faced her, the picture of a submissive patient.

They both greeted me, but Jillian stuck to her business, addressing Walter.

"Let's see how your grip is." She took his hands in hers the same way I'd seen Walter's physician do when he'd tested Walter's grip after the stroke.

"Now squeeze hard with both hands."

Walter squeezed. He and Jillian exchanged a smile.

"You're holding back, aren't you?" she said.

Walter's grin grew a bit bigger, his eyes apologetic. "I didn't want to hurt you."

Jillian pronounced her diagnosis. "He has pretty much full strength in both hands now."

"Would you mind walking for us a bit?" she said.

"If you folks haven't anything better to do than watch me stroll back and forth." He leaned forward and pushed himself out of the chair.

I tried to check with Jillian, wondering whether I should be ready to catch him if he stumbled. She seemed unconcerned, her arms crossed as she watched Walter shuffle to the door and back to his chair.

He raised both hands waist high. "Tada!"

A week before he'd managed just a few feet with the aid of two people, but his gate had become nearly normal, for a sedentary man in his eighties.

Walter seemed to be studying me when I stopped watching his feet and caught sight of his laughing eyes. "Well, how do you explain that?"

I chuckled. "How indeed?"

After we all settled back down, Jillian stuck around for the start of Walter's next dream narration.

Seated in his recliner, Walter took a sip of water then began. "The disciples made a ring around the teacher as he reached a low rock suitable for rest. They were explaining to those waiting that the teacher was tired and needed to sit down for a while to recuperate. They gave him bread and wine and water to refresh him. He took a deep breath and stretched his legs out in front of him, wiggling his toes to loosen them up after so much kneeling and squatting and standing on uneven ground. He flexed his shoulders to loosen them and to relax his neck and back.

"When he had rested for a couple of minutes, he stood and

pushed his friends ahead of him, James and John in the lead. With his hands and his voice, he urged them to walk toward the lake. They wound their way through the crowd until he asked James and John to step aside. They had reached a group of Levites standing together, two older men with priestly tassels on their robes, and a group of younger men and boys who accompanied them.

"'You have brought these to be healed?' The teacher addressed one of the old priests, indicating the group of young men and boys standing and sitting around him.

"'Yes, teacher, these are some of the boys and young men from our clan, the ones who cannot serve in the temple because of blemishes and defects.'

"The teacher nodded. His warm gaze and peaceful smile radiated sympathy toward the men before him.

"'You, who would serve my Father in the temple, have desired the most important thing. And my Father doesn't withhold such blessings from his children.' He raised his hands toward those would-be priests and prayed what I understood to be the traditional prayer of priestly consecration. The men and boys before him stared breathlessly or bowed their heads. First two of the older ones made small, restrained exclamations, then another, and then three in quick succession. The teacher didn't touch any of them. Instead, he held up his hands as a sign of blessing and prayed through that traditional Hebrew prayer. When he reached the Amen, every one of those Levitical heirs stood demonstrating or exclaiming about being healed from his blemish or deformity, from birthmarks to missing fingers, from uneven legs to cleft lips. He healed them all.

"When he finished, a brief pause was shattered by a great shout from the group of men around him. They shouted inarticulate praise and turned to show their friends, brothers, or fathers what had happened to them.

"'Thank you, teacher,' one said. 'May the King of Heaven bless you, teacher,' another said. 'Praise God for blessing his servants through his anointed one,' said the eldest of the priests,

And He Healed Them All

the one who had brought his followers, sons, and nephews to see the teacher.

"The teacher clasped hands with the old priest, and they embraced.

"At that moment a woman pushed her way through the men and boys. She patted one young man on the cheek and smiled through tears at another. She carried a basket under one arm. Bowing her head, she flexed her knees. 'Teacher, thank you for what you've done for our husbands and brothers and sons. Thank you for blessing our clan and our whole village.' She presented him with the basket. 'These are raisin cakes, and honey cakes for you and your disciples.'

"The teacher's friends couldn't rival the cheers of the priests, but they were very thankful for the food. Some of them pushed Matthew toward the teacher and the basket. 'Get him some first; he's weak without food,' Andrew said; and Matthew, quite pale and uncommunicative, shuffled through the crush to where the teacher was pulling cakes out of the basket, which Peter now held. Matthew reminded me, in his blank stare and slow movements, of the way my brother used to be when his blood sugar was low.

"'Matthew.' Peter handed him a raisin cake.

"The teacher caught the cake as Matthew fumbled it. The teacher held the cake steady for Matthew to take a bite of it. When the shaky tax collector took that first bite—even as he began to chew it—his eyes widened and he stood up straight, obviously revived. Then he stopped chewing and looked at the teacher, who still held up the raisin cake. Matthew smiled as if he had just discovered a trick that had been played on him.

"Peter and the others clapped Matthew on the back, and said things like, 'What took you so long?' and 'You should have had him feed you a long time ago.' The teacher smiled amidst the teasing and celebration. But a commotion about fifty yards from where he stood seized his attention.

"Several women wailed. A cloud of dust rose as a dozen men pushed and shouted, maneuvering into position around someone or something. It was too crowded and too far away to see what was taking place. 'Bartholomew, go check on that, please,' the teacher said.

"Bartholomew hurried toward the commotion.

"As the teacher finished healing the cleft lip of a little girl, Bartholomew returned, with another man following him. 'Teacher, a boy has fallen into a crevice among some rocks over there. He seems to be stuck fifteen or twenty feet below the surface.'

"The teacher patted the head of the little girl with the healed lip as her mother thanked him. He headed through the crowd to where the disturbance was still growing. A dozen people shouted instructions to men who had lowered a rope into the crevice, looking like a city work crew dressed in ancient attire.

"I expected that the teacher was there to heal the boy of his injuries when he was rescued. But the rescue attempt proved ineffective, the rope was pulled by several hands out of the hole with no one clinging to the other end. When the teacher arrived, three men were arguing about how to extricate the boy. Apparently they had learned that the boy was lodged between some rocks that had fallen into the hole with him. The argument stopped when the boy's mother begged the teacher to rescue her son.

"'My little boy is stuck down there! He's hurt. Please, please help us!' She wailed.

"'Peace, Mother. We will get him out without any harm. Tell me his name.'

"'He is Jacob.' She clenched her hands together and covered her mouth.

The teacher got down on his knees and braced himself against rocks on both sides of the small split in the mountain. He looked into the darkness for a moment. 'Jacob.'

"A faint voice echoed up.

"The teacher pushed himself up from the crevice and looked around until he saw the rope they had been using for the rescue attempt. He pulled the rope free from the tangle of legs crowded around him and motioned for the people to move back a little.

"One of the men who had been arguing when the teacher arrived stepped up to him. 'You can't just pull him out; his legs are caught among the rocks. When you pull, it hurts him, and he lets go of the rope.'

"The teacher nodded. 'I understand.'

"He turned back to the hole and spoke to the boy once again. 'Jacob, I'm going to raise you out of the hole. Just take hold of this rope I'm lowering to you. You don't need to pull on it, just take hold of it with one hand.'

"Those instructions seemed ridiculous. If the men couldn't pull him out by their rope without hurting him, why bother to lower the rope again? How could he be raised by just one hand? Some of the men began to argue these points, but the mother of the boy stopped them. 'Let the teacher do this. He has done many things today that you couldn't do. Can't he rescue my son as well?'

"I wouldn't have argued with that impenetrable logic, and neither did the men watching the teacher. But they continued to look on with furrowed brows and folded arms.

"'Now just take hold of the rope and don't worry,' the teacher said, after lowering one end.

"He began pulling the rope up hand over hand. I expected to hear the boy cry out in pain, but there was none of that. In fact, the teacher seemed to be pulling up nothing but the rope, he raised it with so little effort. Instead of a cry of pain, we heard the boy complaining, the clarity of his voice growing: 'My legs are stuck. How will you get me out just by holding on to this rope? The rocks are—' He stopped suddenly when he saw the face of the teacher. He looked like he had forgotten what he had been saying.

"The teacher gave Jacob his hand and helped him out of the lip of the crevice. The boy's mouth hung wide open and he peered back into the hole as if he could find an explanation there. Finally, he found words. 'How did you do that?

"The teacher tipped his head slightly. 'Does it really matter?' He patted Jacob on the shoulder. 'Are you hurt?'

"Jacob looked down at his feet, which had been wedged into the rocks. They were bloody and dirty. The teacher knelt and touched the big toe of each foot. 'You are healed.'

And He Healed Them All

"Jacob shook each foot, as if trying to get something off of them, or perhaps waking them up from falling asleep. His mother knelt and poured water on his feet. The dirt washed away as did the blood. And she could find no cuts, or even scratches.

"The teacher moved away from the dangerous crevice, but not before leaving some instructions. 'Block off that hole so no one else falls in.'

"As he pushed into the crowd, the teacher seemed drawn to two young men who were supporting, or perhaps restraining, an older man whose head snapped from left to right, his hands flying to defend his face from invisible attackers. The two younger men attempted repeatedly to capture his hands, and even to keep him from running away. As the teacher approached, one of them said, 'Father, this is he; this is the teacher. He can help you.'

"At this the teacher stepped up to the old man and took hold of his head. Given his state before that, I would have expected this action to provoke more insane behavior. Instead, the old man grasped each arm of the teacher.

"'Oh, yes. I see now. I know now. Thank you. Thank you,' he said, as if the hands of the teacher spoke to him. No words had yet passed the lips of the healer, who simply held the shaggy white head.

"'Let it be restored to you, all that the locusts have eaten, all that the fires burned. Let it all be restored to you,' the teacher said. And then just like that, he moved on.

"The two sons waited for their father, with questions on their faces, as if the old man could explain what the teacher had done. Their father looked first at one and then the other. 'My boys!' he exclaimed, as if he had just returned from a long journey, if only a trip through the tangled land of his own addled mind.

"The teacher approached a young man who had only one hand. Instead of another healthy arm and hand, a pointy sort of stump abbreviated his left arm. Only one bone of his forearm had grown to a natural length, it appeared. He held up the stump for the teacher to see, not hiding it from public view.

"The teacher took hold of the elbow of that arm and held it

up so that the pointed stump rose above the man's head. The man was tall, so hundreds of people could see the malformed arm. For almost a half a minute the teacher held the arm in that position, and nothing appeared to happen. But then the arm suddenly seemed to sprout like a young plant. Out of that first sprout grew a bud and out of that bud branches. In a matter of seconds the healer created a complete hand out of an unfinished arm.

"Just as hundreds could clearly see what was happening, so it was hundreds who exclaimed at the sight of the miraculous creation of a hand out of nothing. Those too far away joined in the noise with their questions: 'What happened?'

"The tall man wrapped his other arm around the teacher and hugged his shoulders while he pumped his new hand in the air. Tears flowed down his face as he sobbed and laughed.

"The power of that healing rippled out to those who saw it.

"I watched as several dozen people seemed to receive spontaneous healings at the very sight of the creation of the hand, and these were either celebrating with their friends and family, worshipping with loud shouts and singing, or falling to the ground out of apparent emotional overload. But those who still had their wits about them moved out of the way so that the teacher could reach others who still needed his touch.

"As I had come to expect, that astonishing visible miracle ignited a sort of healing momentum that accelerated what had already been happening. The teacher seemed energized by its rolling force and began moving more briskly from one person to another. I got the impression that he was trying to seize the moment, that he saw healings about to happen, teetering on the verge, and he moved quickly to tip them over the edge.

"Many reacted physically before he reached them. Others were transformed from sickly to robust health at the slightest touch. A middle-aged man yelled, grabbed at his chest, and then chattered that his pain had disappeared. A woman with a bandaged foot plopped down on the ground to unwind the bandage after the briefest touch from the teacher's hand. A little boy ran in circles and leaped and shouted about his leg growing and his back pain disappearing, even though a knot in the crowd detained the teacher, who could only look at the boy. But a look was evidently enough to send his healing.

"Though his progress through the gyrating crowd was slow and uneven, the teacher appeared quite pleased with the results. His friends, however, scowled in the midst of the bumping, the blocking, and the general noise and chaos.

"The center of the crowd had devolved into something of a healing riot. And the teacher encouraged it, stirring it up by looking for people who needed healing and getting to them as soon as he and his bodyguards could manage. Peter and the others expertly navigated the crowd, uninhibited about pushing through to get where they wanted to go."

Walter stopped and took a long drink of water. Jillian had gone back to her work several minutes before.

Walter chortled. "I have to admit that I still view these dreams in search of proof that they're real, accurate in what they show about Jesus and his healing ministry."

Though his field was sociology of religion, I knew Walter had lately dedicated himself to analyzing the New Testament healing stories, to check his dreams against those accounts of the ministry of Jesus and his followers.

"So what have you concluded?"

He cleared his throat. "A lot of what's most compelling in these dreams is the personal reactions of these people that constituted a pretty anonymous crowd in the Gospel accounts." He reached over and tapped his Bible. "We have individual healing stories, of course, like Lazarus being raised from the dead, for example. But where it says a whole multitude gathered and Jesus had compassion on them and healed them, or healed them all, we don't get to see those individual stories.

"For me, what happens to the people in the dreams feels consistent with those individual healings we read about in the Bible. And it's also consistent with the remarkable assertion that he healed everyone in a large multitude. The variety of ailments would be vast. Moreover, no matter what they were, he healed them all."

I nodded. "I just assumed that you'd find consistency between your dreams and what's written in the Bible. I know you too well to think that you were fabricating the dreams."

Walter's eyes sparkled. "I'm glad you're taking these dreams seriously, and that it's making a difference for you."

I thought about the difference they were making, both healing Walter and reinvigorating his faith, not to mention providing a bridge to Jillian. But along with all of that, I recognized a sort of resistance whirling around inside me.

"The revelation in your dreams isn't a completely peaceful experience for me." I struggled to put words to a feeling I'd been avoiding. "It feels like this fresh wind of grace is swirling against another wind going the opposite direction."

Walter turned his head slightly, a quick little motion of attention and concern. "What's that about?"

I sucked in a deep breath and let it out slowly. "I guess this is shaking up my status quo. It's like part of me wants to just ignore this picture of God invading the world and go back to living like I'm the one in charge of my life."

Walter nodded, recognition stilling his vigilance. "Well, at least it's only *part* of you now?"

I smiled. I guess that *was* progress.

Chapter Ten
Better Late than Never

I arrived at Walter's room much later than usual on Tuesday, barely catching the end of public visiting hours. Walter had finished dinner and was standing by his chair when I reached his door.

"Jillian has come and gone already. You're gonna have to move faster to keep up with that one."

"Long-winded faculty meeting today," I said. I knew Walter understood that phenomenon.

"Well, I'm all out of wind already myself, but you can listen to some of what I recorded about last night's dream, if you like."

"Okay." This was the first I'd heard of the new dream.

Walter stepped toward the door. "I want a change of scenery. Let's go to that little waiting area by Jillian's office and watch for snow through those big windows. You can play back the recording. Who knows, I may want to add something the second time around." He led me through the door and out into the hall.

When we arrived at our destination, I arranged two of the cushy, brown fabric, chairs toward the tall picture windows. We both dropped to our seats wearily, me from a long day of work and Walter from a long life of living.

Walter pressed play on the recorder.

His familiar voice, sounding a bit less full and sonorous, began the narrative: "The vast crowd churning around the teacher offered opportunity to those most determined to reach him. Three men stood before the teacher. They wore long, dark-red cloaks, which were unusual given the weather. They might have intended these cloaks as a bit of a disguise over the Roman military clothing they wore, though I doubt that would work even for someone seeing them at a distance.

"Here was the enemy.

"Two of the men supported the one in the center, who appeared to be older and of higher rank, based on what I could see of the emblems on his armor. He favored his right leg and winced at every step. The teacher looked at him with the same concern and intensity as anyone who had come before. The wounded man didn't look down his nose at this Jewish rabbi, but actually appeared a lot like a boy coming to his father for help. He must have seen healing offered freely to all kinds of people. Apparently he had no fear that the teacher would stop with him.

"The officer tipped his head to the teacher.

"'What happened to your leg?'

"The two soldiers with him suddenly seemed to find the ground fascinating, casting their eyes downward. But the officer answered plainly.

"'We were sent to stop a rebellion in the hills not far from here. The rebels took us by surprise as we rode toward what we understood to be their stronghold. I was hit by a spear; it penetrated my leg.'

"The teacher would certainly have known that the rebels in this account must have been his countrymen, the wound inflicted by a Jewish patriot protecting his land from the foreign invaders. But he appeared to take no thought regarding the political implications. He motioned for the officer to show him the leg.

"Infection had taken hold, so that the leg was nearly double the size of his other. The spear had cut straight through the thigh, halfway up. From the angle, it seemed that it must have at least nicked the bone on the way through. He couldn't bend it at all because of the swelling. That the man was standing could only be attributed to pride and foolish machismo, which I assumed was as much a part of being a Roman officer as the armor.

"After the teacher saw the condition of the leg, he actually seemed concerned, or perhaps troubled is the better word. He didn't touch the leg, nor did he touch the officer. He seemed to be waiting for something.

"A man from the crowd spoke up, a large man with a scar across his nose. He pushed his way past two people in front of him, scowling and pointing to the injured man. 'It's a Roman officer! Look at the way he's dressed. It's a Roman officer seeking healing from his wounds!'

"But who was he accusing—the officer for the audacity to ask the Jewish rabbi to heal his battle wound, or the teacher for not turning him away?

"The teacher peered at the accuser, who now stood close enough that he could know he was right about the identity of the wounded man.

"'Yes, it is as you say. But what is that to you?'

"The accuser turned beet red. He clenched his fists and flexed his jaw muscles, as if warming up for his response. 'He's the enemy! He kills our people to make us slaves to his pagan emperor!'

"The clarity and accuracy of this assessment couldn't be denied. But the teacher added another consideration. 'He is a sinner.'

"The accuser stomped his feet and fairly trembled, his rage shaking him. 'He is the worst kind of sinner, he is—'

"Other voices added their own accusations.

"The teacher cut them off. 'Worse than whom?'

"The accuser fell silent. Muffled replies from the crowd diminished and faded.

"'Worse than you?' The teacher persisted.

"Again the protester offered no response.

"'Who judges which sinners, and which sins, are the worst? How great must a sin be before it negates the power of God to heal? Should I heal only the sinless ones among you? Or should I heal only those with no blood on their hands? What about sexual impurity? Should I heal only the virgins with pure hearts and minds? What is it to you if my Father in heaven is generous to those who don't deserve it?'

"The teacher waited half a moment, then turned to the officer. 'You may go. Your leg is healed.'

"The officer bent over slightly and moaned; then he looked down at his leg and gingerly put his weight on it. He pushed the cloak back to inspect the injury. His leg looked normal in size and color.

"'Thank you, teacher.' A hint of emotion, verging on tears, leaked into his voice. After several bows, he and his soldiers turned and made their way through the crowd to where other soldiers stood with their horses.

"The man who had accused the Roman remained silent. He now faced a dilemma. He stood holding the hand of a little girl he'd brought to be healed. How could he trust his little girl to this traitorous rabbi? Yet, where else could he go? I could see in this man's quandry, another reminder of the remarkable variety of people drawn together in this crowd. More than by social class, nationality, or religious sect, their very understanding of the healing they received from the teacher divided them, as this man's protest demonstrated.

"The teacher solved the accusing man's dilemma to some extent by simply reaching through two rows of people and gently touching the child on the head, at which point her severely crossed eyes instantly straightened. The change was so profound that the militant man dropped any other agenda and hugged his little girl, laughing slightly, while restraining tears, just like the Roman officer had after his healing.

"As the teacher watched the man turn to retreat through the crowd, I noticed that there seemed to be an unusual concentration of children in this part of the hillside. I could sort out what looked like two large families and an additional group of children herded there by one woman.

"The teacher turned to a child from one of the large families. A small boy, about five years old, watched the teacher from his perch in the arms of a woman I assumed to be his mother. The boy's round face framed attentive eyes. The teacher took him

And He Healed Them All

from his mother's arms and gently lowered him to the ground. That's when I saw that his hips were severely misaligned, preventing him from standing normally. Otherwise he appeared quite healthy. He was a stout little boy, but the teacher's strong arms maneuvered him comfortably. It appeared that the teacher healed the boy by gently touching those powerless legs to the ground. The moment his feet bore his full weight, his hips straightened, and a quiver ran through his legs, as if an infusion of strength accompanied the newly aligned hips.

"The round-faced boy looked down at his feet. 'He did it!' He shouted. Then he started to run in circles, around the teacher, around his mother, around his father, then around his brothers and his sisters. The sight of him speeding around drew laughs from all sides.

"Something more remarkable began to happen, however, as the newly motorized boy ran his careening course. Whenever he circled or brushed past a sick or injured child, that child shouted or jumped or began to wave a formerly broken arm or test a formerly deaf ear. The enthusiasm of that running celebration seemed to spread the healing out from the one little boy onto all of the children around him. After the first few were healed, some of them took up the race and began to follow the first little boy, running around and around in circles, weaving in and out among the people, with special attention to the children near them. Within less than two minutes, more than a dozen little children had begun running around and shouting 'He did it!' They coalesced into a high-speed caravan moving as one. Even with so many small boys and girls running wildly, they managed not to crash into one another, nor to trip the adults around them, and this beneficent mayhem continued to spread.

"The teacher just watched. I don't know if I'll ever see so much joy in one face as long as I live. He seemed to be no longer the master of the situation but the most enthusiastic fan instead. He clapped his hands and laughed as the winding race healed new little ones who then joined to run in and out of the crowd. And the healing began to sweep up adults as well. More men and women began to dance with the joy of their healing or that of a loved one.

"After a few minutes, the first boy collapsed to the ground, panting with his eyes closed. And another fell near him, and another landed near the woman with the large, mixed batch of children.

"I overheard someone standing near me say, 'This is the widow that has devoted herself to caring for all of the orphans in this area.'

"The caregiver stood weeping joyfully with both hands held over her mouth. It was then that I guessed that the teacher had orchestrated this display for her. He had released the miraculous celebration to bless that woman who had turned from the sorrow of her loss to helping the smallest of the needy ones around her. The teacher smiled at her with tears in his eyes. She smiled back as she received the wonderful blessing he poured out for her. After all, he could have just healed the children one at a time, as he did with most of the people in the crowd that day. But this playful display of healing grace shone bright even in that day full of good news.

"The running children continued to drop out, exhausted, laughing, and panting. They exercised limbs and senses that had only cursed them before. Among them sat a girl, about six or seven, with light brown hair. She sat in the ragged grass on the sunbaked hill, examining her pink hands as if receiving sight for the first time.

"Once again I could see the teacher hesitate, as if he wanted to just stay there among those deliriously happy children, but he tore himself away from these inspiring little ones and again offered healing to all those who came to him.

"A middle-aged woman presented a heavily bandaged arm to him. She started to unwrap it to show him some festering sore that had stained that crude covering a rusty color, but he stopped her, clasped her face between his hands, and kissed her on the forehead. She made almost a barking sound in surprise at this manner of blessing, but then she stared at her bandaged arm. She rapidly unwound the bandage just in time to watch the last of the sore disappearing under new skin.

"A tall, thin woman moved to the teacher. Her red nose and watery, swollen eyes spoke of a severe cold or allergy. Her face bore lines that hinted that this condition was chronic, and her weary posture testified to surrendered hope.

"The teacher placed his hands gently on her cheeks. Her eyebrows arched suddenly and she said, 'Oh,' and smiled at the teacher. Her eyes no longer held a tired, glassy look, and her nose was no longer red and runny. She took a deep breath through her nose and chuckled broadly. 'Thank you,' she said with obvious relief.

"Two men carried a cot to a small opening in the crowd when the healed woman stepped away. On the cot lay a man who couldn't have weighed more than a hundred pounds, and most of that in bones that stood out prominently. I wondered how a man lived so long as to get to this wasted condition in a time when medical care was as often harmful as helpful.

"The teacher knelt by the cot and took the hand of the skeletal man. Their eyes locked, as if each had been waiting to meet the other, and now neither could be distracted from the experience of longing fulfilled. The strong hand of the teacher helped the man to sit up on his cot. It looked impossible. How could this frail man, who appeared beyond death's door, sit up? Even with the help of the teacher, it appeared that this simple exertion spent all of his energy.

"The teacher steadied him and then instructed the stretcher bearers to place the cot on the ground. The man remained sitting, even when the teacher let go of his hand. I'm sure a strong wind would have knocked him over. His two friends stayed near, lest he should totter.

"The teacher turned to the next person waiting, who seemed to be feverish, for he was flushed, his eyes drooping and a slow, labored pace to his movements. The teacher touched the man's forehead. His color turned cooler and his eyes cleared; he stood erect as the fever apparently abated.

"The teacher returned to the man on the cot. While my attention had been distracted, the sitting man had grown somewhat steadier, as if sitting was no longer such a challenge. He even seemed to be less gaunt. Again the teacher took his hand and ventured deep into his eyes. A smile enlivened the face of the man on the cot.

"The teacher turned briefly and healed a very small boy held in somebody's arms, so that the little boy could hear when the teacher tested his ears. When the teacher finished, the little boy began to play at covering and uncovering his ears. Then the teacher turned back to the man on the cot one more time.

"This time the teacher helped him to stand. Reminding me of old documentaries of Holocaust survivors, the thin man still didn't look well, his new posture emphasizing how far he had yet to climb to reach full health.

"The teacher held on a bit longer this time and then let go so that he could take a baby from its mother's arms. He held the baby girl like an experienced mother would, kissing her on the forehead and handing her back to her mother, who grinned and thanked him when she saw that the girl's drooping eyelid had been totally healed. The mother began to shout and wave one hand in the air as she danced away with her baby.

"One last time the teacher returned to the man who had arrived on the cot, but who now stood on his own. His face looked almost normal, still thin, but as healthy as I could have imagined, given what he looked like when he arrived. The teacher embraced him, holding him close, as if that body contact would accelerate the transfer of health from himself to the revived man. When the teacher released him, the man was smiling and standing quite well on his own. As hard as it was for me to believe, the man must have gained forty pounds in those few moments, and certainly whatever it was that had driven him into that wasted condition had passed away from his body. The teacher had healed both the cause and the deadly symptoms.

"After receiving the gratitude of the restored man and his friends, the teacher beckoned for another man to come out of the

And He Healed Them All

crowd to him. This man had a cloth wrapped around his head to cover one eye. 'What happened?'

"'I'm a stonemason. I was working in Jerusalem, cutting stone for Herod's guard house, and a piece of stone flew into my eye. It hurt a lot at first but has gotten even worse, all red and swollen and sore."

"'Remove the bandage.'

"The man complied, going somewhat gingerly toward the end, and needing assistance from the woman standing with him, who might have been his wife. They finally uncovered the infected eye. It was quite inflamed as he had described, with the lid sealed shut. Clearly, the sunlight intensified his pain; he winced and held his hand up to block the sun.

"The teacher stepped close to the man and blew a small puff of breath on the eye. The stonemason's black eyebrows shot up, and I watched as the swelling vanished and the redness disappeared. After a half a minute of blinking against the sunlight, he was looking quite normal, a broad smile stretching across his face. He sighed as if finally able to end his vigil against the pain.

"The next man wore a bandage around his hand, but the injury he had suffered also registered on his downcast and deeply lined face. The teacher asked him about it. 'Why so sad, my friend?'

"'Teacher, I have been heartsick for many days now. I owed a debt to some men who came to collect when I didn't pay on time. I'm a musician; I play stringed instruments in the temple and for celebrations in the city. To avenge my failure to pay my debt, they cut off my fingers.' He fought tears. Awkwardly, with his other hand, he uncovered his mangled hand. Those who had maimed him had not been particularly efficient about their work. One finger still dangled grotesquely; it had turned black and stiff as it died there.

"People standing nearby recoiled or averted their eyes. The teacher stayed put, shaking his head. He gently cradled the musician's hand in his own. Then he briefly licked his own index finger on the opposite hand and touched the dead finger.

"That finger responded by changing color and then twisting and snapping into place, the tenuous connection replaced by a normal joint. The musician stared with his mouth stuck halfway open. He began to quiver uncontrollably, as if in shock.

"The teacher spoke directly to the amputated fingers. 'Grow.' And they did. It took ten seconds for the newly sprouted fingers to grow out of the mangled joints that remained from his punishment. Like all of us, the musician stared wide-eyed. Still shaking, he began to flex his fingers and then made the motion of plucking strings. He laughed like a drunken man.

"'Even better than before!' And his laughter grew more hysterical. He staggered away without thanking the teacher.

"While most people walked away after being healed, many stayed to watch. Others rejoiced, dancing and singing in celebration of all that they had experienced for themselves, as well as what they'd witnessed being given to others. The widow and her band of orphans, for example, had stayed to worship and watch. Because there was still a press of people waiting to be healed, the watchers and worshippers had to move off to one side to avoid restricting access to the teacher. But no one watched without waves of emotion registering on their faces, like a large family watching their children open presents at Christmas, only far better."

Walter clicked off the recorder and turned back to the snow falling outside before he faced me.

I knew by then that I needed him to comment on the dreams. For me, Walter was not just the receiving vessel; he was the chief interpreter.

"These scenes are very dramatic. People falling down, crying out, and such," I said.

Walter nodded. "All I can say about that is it all seems so natural in the context. How would you respond to being instantly healed of a long-term illness?"

I laughed and shook my head slowly as I stared out the window. "That's so far beyond my experience that I'm sure I have no idea." I had been thinking about this emotional aspect of such dramatic healings, the impact of tangibly seeing one's own body healed or that of someone close. But, to be honest, it was easier for me to treat the dreams as someone else's story, muting its impact on me.

"I know my own dramatic improvement has meant more than just better mobility and table manners," Walter said, winking at me. "The infusion of hope and joy is more than I've ever experienced."

Though I knew that Walter was speaking honestly, I was struck by the contrast with his former reserve regarding matters of faith. I recalled a time when I was at his house when two young men knocked at the door. This was maybe fifteen years ago. I sat in a chair in the living room as Walter answered the door out of my line of sight. My first thought was that these were Jehovah's Witnesses, but they introduced themselves as part of a new Baptist church in town. I listened from the other room, interested in his response to their sales pitch.

"We'd love to have you come and visit our church some time. Everyone is welcome," the clear and bouncy voice of one young man said.

I could hear Walter shuffling uncomfortably on the wooden floor in front of his door. "No, I'm already part of a church, and have been for nearly fifty years."

"Oh, well that's great to hear," the other religious solicitor said.

To me his expanded reply sounded a bit rehearsed. "We're not interested in stealing people away from any other church if you're completely happy with it. Would you say that you're happy with the church you now attend?"

"Happy?" Walter's voice peaked incredulously. "I'd say satisfied." Then he rumbled the conversation to a stop. "I'm not looking for a change of any kind."

Before either of the young men could start his follow-up, Walter added, "So, I wish you a good afternoon. I don't have any more to say."

I heard the door close a half second later. I pictured the two young men standing outside the door, looking at it with their mouths gearing up for the next bit of their spiel. I smiled to myself at how easily Walter had let them off. As a sociologist specializing in comparing religious experiences, he certainly could have educated those young men if he was inclined to argue. I watched him walk slowly into the living room, tucking his white cotton shirt and hiking up his pants as he often did when he was nervous.

"Not interested in converting?" I teased him.

"'Are you happy with your current church?'" He quoted the solicitor incredulously. "I don't think happy and church go together for most people, do you?"

At the time I was still attending a big nondenominational church on the edge of town. "Well, I think my church makes my teeth whiter and keeps me looking younger."

Walter had laughed at my joke. "You might want to hit the streets and see if you can sell that door-to-door. But I'll just stick with what I know and leave the happiness to the advertising agencies."

Neither of us laughed about church and religion these days. "This isn't the way you used to talk about your faith," I said, glancing at him before turning back to the winter scene outside.

He nodded. "You noticed that, did you? Yep, this is a whole new experience for me, like I was missing something all these years and didn't even know it."

I smiled as if I understood, but I felt like a bit of a phony, affirming Walter's transformation while still keeping myself safely out of the way of the passing train that had picked him up. That this train was going somewhere important impressed me less than the fact that it was fast and dangerous.

We silently watched the falling snow sharply illuminated against the dark night. After a couple of minutes, I helped Walter to his feet and walked with him back to his room. There, we talked further about the dreams, until the night nurses good-naturedly threatened to throw me out if I didn't leave voluntarily.

Chapter Eleven
Weary from Doing Good

By that Thursday, I had begun to accept a sort of push and pull between my accustomed academic life and the living Gospel contained in Walter's dreams. From my peak of resolve the week before, when I dined with Jillian at my house and then went to church with her, I had sunk back into my routines, and not just the ordinary daily tasks, but also my ordinary way of thinking. In that mode, I generally relegated God to backstage with the rest of the old props from my childhood, gathering dust in the darkness.

Driving through a cold fog that left a sheen on the trees and sidewalks, I gingerly made my way to see Walter, careful about the condition of the roads. Still distracted by my dissatisfaction, I drifted into hoping that Walter had another dream to tell me, for in the middle of those stories, I knew what was important and lasting, and I wanted those things, at least in those moments.

When I passed the nurse's station, pulling off my coat and shaking off the dampness, I slowed my pace at the sight of Walter talking to a white-haired woman just outside his door. I kept my distance in order to avoid interrupting, not feeling very friendly just then. In fact, I felt completely out of sorts.

Their conversation ended, Walter patted her on the shoulder and she turned to scuff across the carpet in her bedroom slippers. I was relieved to escape pretending to be amiable.

Walter looked up at me, apparently a bit startled by my arrival.

"Oh, James. I didn't see you there. But I guess it's that time."

"Yep, your supper's over and my day at school is too," I said.

I followed him into his room; he offered me a seat and took his place in the big easy chair, reaching over to adjust a piece of notepaper with pencil scrawling on it.

"My notes from the latest dream. I did record it, but wanted notes here in case I had time to tell you about it."

I sat in his guest chair and sighed expansively. "There's nothing I want more now than to relax and listen to another one of your dreams."

He looked at me for an extra moment, perhaps noting my mood and assessing a possible response. Instead of directly addressing my muted manner, he glanced at his notes and began recalling the dream from the night before.

"By now the teacher was beginning to lean on his friends extensively, and he moved more slowly both hand and foot. He must have touched, talked to, and even struggled with thousands of people in that day. As the sun inched toward the horizon, the teacher walked with helpers on each side, the two brothers, James and John. These two stood shoulder to shoulder with him, hands at the ready. They allowed him to lean against them when he stopped to touch blind eyes or when he opened deaf ears. They helped raise him after he bent down to touch a crippled person lying at his feet, their hands steadying the teacher without apparent strain or awkwardness. They had obviously done this before.

"The one who brought healing and freedom to a crowd of several thousand now showed his own humanity. But the healing didn't stop. Nor did his physical weariness cause him to struggle to heal. If anything, the miracles came more freely, more surprisingly.

"In this condition, he stood over a woman who sat on the ground weeping, occasionally pounding the ground with her open hands and gasping for breath. Next to her lay the motionless form of a child. It appeared to me that the girl was dead, her face ashen, her body shriveled for one so young. Though it was hard to tell exactly, she seemed about ten years old. The uninhibited grief of the woman next to her led me to believe that this must be the mother.

"The teacher paused above the still form of the little girl while the woman wailed. To my surprise, a great sob burst from the teacher's lips. James turned sharply to him. Evidently, he too was surprised at this reaction. I glanced at John, however, who was also crying, tears trickling down his cheeks and into his beard. Perhaps the source of John's sorrow was the nasty irony that this little girl had apparently died here in this crowd of people pushing toward the teacher, the greatest source of healing the world had ever encountered. In the presence of hope and healing, this little girl and her mother found death instead.

"At the teacher's sob, the woman looked up. For a moment she didn't seem to recognize him, staring blankly at this man propped between two other strangers. But I think the way the crowd stood focused on the teacher and his followers awakened her to the identity of this man weeping sympathetically for her.

"I wondered whether she could forgive him for failing to save her girl. Before her stood a man whose own body had begun to pay a toll for the long day. But all I saw from the forlorn woman was deep loss and sadness

"The crowd had made room for the mother and child on the ground, leaving a void for the grief of this ultimate loss. They stood silently watching as the teacher waded into that pool of sorrow.

"With two or three more sobs and some broken words and gestures, the teacher directed James and John to help him down next to the grieving mother. For a moment, the teacher sat next to her, making a matched pair of mourners, both looking at the little girl's perfectly still body. In that moment, it seemed to me that this healer was not simply grieving the death of this one little girl. Perhaps he wept for other mothers and their dead, and dying, children over the whole country, even the world. Did he know them all? Did he grieve for them all?

"Wiping away his tears, he gestured for his friends to help him back to his feet. As he stood, he said to the woman, 'Pick up your child, Mother; she will be hungry.'

"The mother looked up at him, a sob frozen in her mouth. She jerked her head toward her daughter.

"From where I watched, it looked as if the ground had moved around the child. Not an earthquake, but a swelling of the earth, as if it took a breath and released it.

"Blindly obedient, the woman slid her shaking arms beneath the head and legs of her fawn-like daughter. She drew the little body to her and startled as the corpse awakened to life. Instead of removing a body, she now embraced her living daughter.

"The universe had moved and life had returned to wake the dead. And the girl didn't merely make a small step back from death to life; rather, she received total healing from whatever sickness had taken her life. The once lifeless girl now hugged her mother vigorously. The mother's weeping surrendered spaces for laughter and praise, while her little girl just held on and smiled. The crowd had erupted into cheers when they saw the child revive.

"Beneath that din, the girl said something in her mother's ear that halted her sobbing and laughter. They both looked at the teacher, who leaned on his friends. The mother released the little girl, who stood up and stepped over to him, reaching out to take his hand. He smiled at her and seemed to gain strength from her touch, her little hand in his. He stood taller. In a muted voice he said, 'Thank you, my girl,' and smiled weakly as he turned to address the next person waiting to be lifted out of despair. But the woman he turned to, out of the whole array of people standing there around him, looked rather embarrassed, avoiding eye contact and keeping her large, middle-aged face bowed toward the ground.

"The teacher addressed her. 'What would you have me do for you, sister?'

"She glanced at the woman holding her resurrected daughter. 'I don't need nothin' important, really. I just was hopin' for my hair to grow back.' She nearly whispered the answer. She lifted her head covering just enough to give the teacher a peek.

"He leaned forward and gently kissed her forehead. 'Then let it be so.'

"When the teacher kissed her, her eyes got big and she giggled. Then she furrowed her brow and scratched her head through the covering. She poked her finger under the cloth then stuck her hand in. The rough veil fell away to her shoulders. A beautiful head of thick and healthy hair cascaded over her neck and back.

"'Oh, my!' She cackled. 'I never had hair like this even when I was young!'

"Indeed, he had blessed her with a luxurious head of hair, lavishing on her an abundance. She shook her head so that the locks of new hair fell forward where she could see them better. Then she blushed quite red at this immodest display of her own beauty. I remembered then that it says somewhere in Scripture that long hair is a woman's glory. That simple woman seemed to believe it and had new reason to celebrate it. But she mustered enough restraint to pull her head covering back into place before she thanked the teacher and turned to join the worshippers dancing nearby.

"I had noticed the teacher looking at a barrel-chested man in the crowd before each of the last two healings. Now this man stood within reach.

"The teacher addressed him. 'Benjamin.'

"'Yeshua,' Benjamin said in return. He moved toward the teacher but hesitated briefly. The teacher held open his arms. They hugged like reunited friends.

"'How are things in Nazareth?' the teacher said.

"'As before, of course. You know that nothing changes in Nazareth.'

"The teacher laughed. 'It's good that you've come. The power to heal is here today, as you can see. This remote place is at the center of God's eye, and you are, of course, welcome to all that the Father has prepared for us here.'

"Benjamin raised his right arm a few inches and reached across to that shoulder with his left, a grimace enveloping his face. 'This is all the motion I have in this shoulder. I can't farm her grabbed hold of the ailing shoulder and I heard bystanders winced at the sound, but Benjamin laughed a high-pitched laugh. 'Hee, hee, oh, that's much better!' He rotated the shoulder.

"Even as the teacher smiled back, Benjamin's face straightened. 'You should come back and give them another chance.'

"'I will do that when the time is right. Pass my greetings to friends and family back home.'

"The men embraced again before Benjamin merged back into the crowd.

"A woman tapped the teacher. A girl about fourteen years old stood with her. 'My little girl had the most beautiful singing voice—'

"The teacher interrupted her by touching the girl's cheek, just one gentle touch.

"The daughter clutched her throat. 'It's hot.' She trembled from head to foot. Her mother startled. She scowled at the teacher, as if somehow put off by the hasty manner of the healing.

"As the mother doted on her daughter, the teacher turned to a man and woman standing nearby. They wore ragged clothes and were very dirty. They held on to each other, for courage or strength, I wasn't sure. The woman said, 'Sir, my husband has been out of work for a long time, because he can't seem to keep his mind on anything long enough to do any kind of work.' The man nodded, but his expression flashed from childish glee to consternation and back again.

"The teacher took the man's head in his hands and looked at the wild questioning eyes in the sunburned, dirty face. 'What is your name?'

"The man hesitated, but the fluctuation from one extreme facial expression to another ceased. His newly steady eyes examined the teacher, as if he had finally found what he was looking for. 'I'm Mordechai.' His voice was almost childlike.

"'You are free now. Go home and take care of your wife'

"'Yes, sir, I will. Thank you.'

And He Healed Them All

"His wife stood still, looking from the teacher to her husband and back, clearly trying to confirm that something had changed. Finally she focused on Mordechai and met his eyes. The look on her face reminded me of a school girl blushing with affection for a new love. The husband and wife left through the crowd, arm in arm, the wife petting and clinging to Mordechai.

"The girl who had just received healing in her throat began to sing. She sang a song of praise that sounded to me like one of the psalms. Her voice silenced a widening pool of chattering people around her. They stopped to listen and absorb the sweet rain of her voice falling on them. Gradually, other voices joined hers. They sang a poignant song of celebration, perfectly suited to this day so full of joy and restoration."

From the expression on his face, I could easily believe that Walter was still hearing that song as he sat across from me, his feet up and head back in the comfortable recliner. He only managed to break away from that memory for my sake, I think. He lifted his head from the back of the chair.

"It's hard to come back," he said, acknowledging what I had suspected.

After a few moments of resituating himself in his chair and pushing his glasses into place, he seemed to head toward the periphery of his experience, as if in search of some distance.

"One thing I wasn't prepared for is the wide variety of methods, as well as the myriad reactions, to the healings." He spoke as if he was answering a question. "That variety speaks to me of a personal connection. It's as if the teacher knows each person so well that he knows exactly the best way to reach them and to heal their particular injury or sickness."

"In this dream you had another kind of variety," I said. "He raised a little girl from the dead, and then followed that by healing a woman's hair loss. Do you think he really cared about something as minor as baldness?"

Walter laughed and rubbed his bald head, leaving the wispy strands that crossed his shiny skull ruffled and half standing up. "What do you think? Maybe my baldness gets healed when the stroke is all done?"

I grinned, a bit embarrassed at having made the baldness comment.

He answered seriously. "I don't think it's the exact nature of the need that matters. I wish you could see the welcoming intensity that I see in the eyes of the teacher. He looks at everyone as if he knows them, every bit as warm and excited as a father returning home from work greets his toddler." Walter seemed to leave me again, with that transparent look focused on some horizon beyond my perception. "Besides," he said suddenly, "the Bible says 'he healed them all.' That has to include the profound as well as the incidental, doesn't it?"

"Yes, it does," I said. I hadn't been trying to argue a particular point. I was just reaching into that picture of unbounded love that Walter painted, hoping to get a little of it on my hands.

Walter paused a moment and then turned an unexpected corner. "I've been thinking about what to do with these dreams, after I'm gone from this life, I mean."

Some childish vestige in me spoke without editing, as I often did with Walter. "You're not going anywhere any time soon."

Walter frowned and ran his hand over his bald head again, this time settling the few hairs that had continued to reach for the sky. "Actually"—he drew out the word—"I feel pretty sure that I'm not gonna be here much longer, and I don't think that's just something I came up with on my own. I've been praying and asking God about a few things, and getting what I feel like are some pretty clear answers."

I guess I would have expected that Walter prayed, in general. I would have expected him to pray about things that troubled him, or big decisions he needed to make. But I had never heard him refer to prayer as something that was interactive. That idea was a big adjustment to my thinking.

"How do these answers come?" I was truly curious, perhaps even ready to believe him.

"Oh, mostly just ideas that seem too wise and selfless for me to feel like they originated in my head. Just like I get ideas that seem so perverse and destructive that I know they also didn't originate with me."

"Walter, you're stretching me again." I laughed, but I felt anything but humor.

Walter rocked forward, forcing the footrest in his recliner to settle down so that his feet planted firmly on the floor. He leaned forward a bit, a move that used to be beyond his capabilities. Then, to top it off he stood up and held his hands out at his sides, palms up, drawing my attention to his posture. "After this, my whole worldview has stretched to the point of tumbling down like a house of cards. And that's about what it was, I'm beginning to believe, just a house of cards."

Of course, this was Walter's testimony, but it stung me. If his faith before the dreams was a house of cards, what was mine? Maybe just a pile of cards, neglected by some kid who forgot to clean up after himself. Walter rescued me from having to go on confronting my disheveled faith.

"What I was starting to say, earlier," he said, sitting slowly back in his chair, "was that I'd like you to consider writing these dreams in some form, for a wider audience than just the three of us."

I let "the three of us" comment distract me for a minute. To some extent, my emotional universe had narrowed to that same trio: Walter, Jillian, and myself. But then I switched to considering what he was saying about getting the story of the dreams onto paper, to a wider audience.

I nodded and shrugged my shoulders. "I'll consider it. I do think the story should be told. But I think you ought to be the one telling it." I wound up for another appeal. "As you pointed out a minute ago, you're recovering your physical strength, and you're as sharp as ever. Why don't you start writing?"

He tipped his head slightly and waggled his eyebrows. "I don't think they're done yet, so it's too early to start writing an unfinished story."

His response avoided answering my question directly, but I didn't want to press him on the point.

And He Healed Them All

"I wonder if you'll know for sure when it's all over," I said, referring to the dreams, but choosing my words poorly.

Walter smiled. "I think it'll be clear when we get there."

Chapter Twelve
Signs of Passing

Jillian and I visited Walter the following Saturday. Jillian had invited me to a concert, ironically hosted at the big church I used to attend. I agreed, with the caveat that I wanted to see Walter about a dream. She said she had a bit of work to do, so I met her at her office and walked with her down the hall to Walter's room.

She nodded a greeting to one of the nurses as we walked past.

"How often do you come in here on a Saturday?"

Before she could answer me, a pale old man in a wheelchair waved her down, as if stranded on the side of a deserted road late at night. I stopped abruptly and shooed away a bit of resentment as I watched her address him with a steady smile and firm, uninterrupted attention.

"Hello, Mr. Perkins. How are you doing today? Recovered from the surgery?"

I couldn't hear what the old gentleman said. His voice was like gravel in a cement mixer. The movement of his mouth was hindered by a stroke or something, but Jillian leaned in close and seemed to understand his answer. She pulled a stray lock of hair back behind her ear as she bent toward the plaintive patient. He seemed to have some concern about his foot. Jillian followed his bony, shaking hand, which came to rest on his knee after spending another ounce of energy to point to his right foot.

By the time Jillian had satisfied Mr. Perkins's concerns, I had accumulated a small pile of self-rebukes for impatience, resentment, and even a bit of jealousy, as if the watery-eyed old gent had stolen my girlfriend by feigning some kind of health problem at the age of ninety-three. When Jillian turned from Mr. Perkins, she winked at me and put her arm through mine, my hands stuffed into the pockets of my jeans. Could she sense all those ratty feelings I had been chasing away while she worked a bit of overtime caring for a needy old man? I just smiled weakly, avoiding a smoldering thought that she was too good for me.

We walked the remaining yards to Walter's door. When we looked in he was standing by the window, using the late afternoon daylight to read from an old hardcover book.

"James!" He greeted me with a smile that distracted me from my self-condemnation. He smiled at Jillian and gave her a friendly nod. "Doctor."

Then he said the words that I longed to hear during those days. "I had another dream."

By this time, I had developed a bipolar feeling about the growing number of dreams. On the one hand, I wondered how long these could go on. And, on the other hand, I hoped against all likelihood that they would never stop. Of course, this hope probably had something to do with wanting Walter to live on forever.

"So how are classes going?" He asked, as I started to help him walk back to his chair and then remembered that he didn't need my help anymore.

I shook my head. "The students are so alien to me, so different from when I was in school." As soon as I said that, I realized how reminiscent it must sound to my old professor.

Walter laughed, but Jillian pursued my comment.

"How are they different?"

I stopped to consider her question while Jillian climbed onto Walter's bed, which had been lowered to a height that made it easy for him to get in and out.

"They've all grown up in a culture that insists everything must be instant," I said. "I mean, we had our microwaves and our drive-thru restaurants, but information, or even truth, is something they arrive at with the click of a few buttons. And their truth has a hundred heads, all of them equal and none of them satisfying to an old-timer like me."

I scooted the guest chair into position next to the bed and facing Walter. Jillian playfully nudged me with her knee where I pulled up close to her. "'Old-timer.' Pffft."

Walter had settled in and found his notes on the latest dream. They lay next to the digital recorder. I wondered whether the recorder had nearly filled, when Walter spoke, sounding a bit winded.

"Oh, I'm sure you're right, which is why my generation is fortunate to be out of the way. Your generation is the one that gave these kids all the gadgets and ideas they've run away with. Now *you* have to deal with it."

Though his words were somewhat whimsical, his mouth and eyes seemed tight, his voice a bit strained.

Jillian and I glanced at each other; I assumed she too was noting the way his energy seemed to have dissipated.

Walter appeared to notice our exchange and looked at each of us briefly in turn. "Well, you want to hear about the dream?"

We both nodded.

"I'll tell you what I remember.

"I'm recalling a moment when the teacher smiled and took one small step to his left, careful to clear a small rock in his way. On the ground sat an African man, whose ebony skin was marked by nasty sores from his ankles to his forehead. Whatever the cause of the sores, it apparently also sapped his strength.

"A man who appeared to be a Roman or Greek spoke to the teacher. 'Sir, this man is my most beloved servant, like a brother to me, really. Please help him if you can.'

"The teacher motioned for the master to help his servant stand, bypassing any comment on what he *could* do. The master, who was surely a wealthy man, complied readily. He crouched low and, holding both arms from behind, assisted his servant to stand before the teacher. It seemed to me that the only reason for making this weary man stand was simply that it would have been too difficult for the exhausted teacher to kneel or squat on the ground for each person so late in that day.

"When the servant had regained his feet, he bowed respectfully to the teacher, though it was the weak and resigned bow of a man preserving his every grain of strength just to survive. The teacher stepped very close, toe-to-toe, in fact. I think he intentionally allowed his own sandaled toes to touch those of the sick man. Their noses but a few inches apart, the teacher spoke two words softly, but with the conviction of a man who knows his orders will be obeyed: 'Be well.'

"It looked just like a sudden wind had blasted out from the teacher, without any physical effort on his part. The servant flew backward, as from a bomb blast, and his master staggered back into people standing behind him. This healing blast made it appear to me that the man had been blown right out of his sores, as if they had stayed where they were as he was launched clear.

"The tall, handsome servant, supported by his master behind him, shook with a whole body shiver that seemed to come from deep within, eventually filling him like wind in a sail. And he was well, his skin clean of all visible sores, his posture sure and strong.

"A white-toothed smile broke from his face. It was a beautiful sight. But the teacher had moved on to the next person. The servant and his master embraced, each raising a fist to the sky in triumphant celebration as they walked away, arm in arm.

"The teacher merely touched the shoulder of a stooped old woman who was propping herself with a long knotty cane. With loud popping sounds, her back straightened and she threw her head back and uttered one loud 'Ha!' straight up at the sky. Then her whole frame adjusted to the change so that she stood perfectly upright and facing forward. She smiled at John, who was now in front of her, as the teacher stepped to his left again. John blessed her and then followed the teacher.

"Three stretchers lay side-by-side on the ground before the teacher. He looked at the man on his right. 'Get up; you are well.'

"Only after he said this did I look hard at the man and see

that he was no more than a skeleton with skin. This condition changed completely in the space of time required for the sickly man to sit up, gather his legs beneath him, and rise to his feet. The process of standing seemed to take unusually long—prolonged by the fact that there was more happening than just a man getting up off of his bed. Finally, there stood a tall man, taller than the teacher, of a fairly healthy weight, now apparently quite far from the grave that had seemed only moments away when the teacher spoke to him.

"The teacher turned his attention to the next stretcher, where a man wrapped in bandages looked up at the teacher like a child awaiting his mother's care. The teacher reached out his hand and bent his knees slightly. James took hold of the teacher's other arm to support him as the touch of the teacher met the outstretched hand of the bandaged man. When their fingers connected, both the teacher and the prone man began to vibrate, as if taking part in their own private earthquake. The hand of the man on the ground shot up unnaturally. The teacher snapped back to a standing position under the pull from James. John steadied him.

"When the teacher and the bandaged man broke contact, the man on the ground jumped to his feet, bandages fluttering all around him. Those bandages had obviously been wound around a limp and sickly man and didn't survive the movement of the now healthy and vital man. The teacher motioned to James to help get the bandages off, even as two men and a woman, family it seemed, were stepping all over the abandoned stretcher to help with the task.

"During this flurry of activity, I noticed a sudden upward movement to the teacher's left. The third person on a stretcher, a teenage girl, had already stood up and had begun praising God with her hands raised over her head. In one hand she held a roughly fashioned splint that looked like it had supported both of her legs. She was dancing up and down on her stretcher, essentially running in place, as if she couldn't stop herself. The teacher clapped his hands in celebration at the sight of the healing that had gotten ahead of him. The prospect of such spontaneous healings must have looked very good to the weary teacher, who surely wanted to see as many people as possible healed in that day. And what was possible? I wondered.

"James returned to supporting the teacher in another round of touching the sick. Again I thought in terms of momentum. The spontaneous healing of the teenage girl caught the attention of at least one other person. A younger girl, about ten or eleven years old, was flexing her left arm, which had previously been in a sling hung around her neck. She smiled and showed the arm to the teacher. He grinned broadly. 'God is good,' he said.

"She nodded and waved her arm before a woman that I assume was her mother.

"The teacher touched the forehead of a small man standing next to that girl, and the man began coughing as if frantically trying to dislodge some small creature that had flown down his throat. In response, the teacher bent down and said in a low voice, 'Come out.' At that, the coughing ceased and the man stood up straight, taking a deep breath, even spreading his arms out as wide as the crowd would allow, sucking in a lungful of air.

"With unbroken determination, the teacher continued moving, John and James still close beside him. The next woman he approached appeared to be trapped in a deep internal storm, her face contorted, her eyes shifting from left to right. When the teacher touched her forehead, both of her arms shot out in front of her, missing the teacher but forcing both James and John backward. Fortunately, a second level of support, Thaddeus and Andrew, caught the brothers as they stumbled back. The teacher remained unmoved.

"'Shalom,' he said to her. And that word must have carried power and meaning that covered what the woman needed. That storm within her broke, and tears rained. Her dark, unwashed hair fell over her face as she bowed into her catharsis. Two of the women among the teacher's helpers stepped forward and took hold of the crying woman's arms to support her as the teacher moved on.

"In quick succession, the teacher touched and healed a man

with an infection in his gums, a woman with some unspoken ailment and a girl who was deaf in one ear, touching each of them briefly before stepping to the next person. He flowed to his left as the crowd shifted, people moving away when they were healed and others stepping forward. At this point, it seemed that the crowd consisted of an even mixture of people still desperate to get their healing, alongside others simply watching the miracles.

"A middle-aged man gingerly stepped before the teacher. 'I always have this pain in my back, here.' He placed his hand on his lower back.

"'Back pain, be gone!' the teacher said.

"The man suddenly stood up straight. He moved nimbly as he patted his lower back, apparently searching for the point of pain. Behind him, two more people grabbed at their backs, an older woman and a young man barely twenty years old. A trio of exclamations followed as all three discovered new flexibility.

"John gave the teacher some water to drink from a cup and James asked him how he was doing.

"The teacher reassured them. 'I'm fine, my friends. You are doing very well. I appreciate your help.' He patted James on the cheek. I think he was trying to assuage any fears they had regarding how hard he was pushing himself. Surely, he knew how much he could take.

"A woman who appeared to be pregnant was ushered before the teacher by a man holding her arm and supporting her back. 'My wife has a growth inside her. She looks like she's pregnant, but she's not. It's a tumor or growth in her stomach.'

"The teacher nodded then pushed a finger into the growth, which disappeared. The woman belched loudly. She and her husband laughed heartily as her dress fell loosely about her waist.

"A boy with a bandage over his right eye laughed at the woman's impropriety. The teacher touched him. 'Infection, be gone!' The boy clapped his hand to his eye and yanked away the bandage. His eye was perfectly healthy. He laughed, and blinked both eyes several times as if to test them.

"The teacher took advantage of a momentary pause and put

his arm around John to rest himself. He accepted a drink of wine from Joanna, and then stood for a moment, relaxing his whole body as much as possible in a standing position. The crowd pressed closer. Their worried looks led me to believe that his pause in healing may have made them think that he was nearly done, that all the power was about to be spent. In response to this new crush, the teacher's bodyguards joined arms to form a tighter protection around him.

"He rested inside this ring of his followers, ten strong men, sweaty in the late afternoon sun, locked together like a great defensive machine. The teacher moved them with a nod of his head or a gentle push on the back of Peter, who stood directly in front of him. He reached over their protective arms and touched the next sick or injured person.

"My attention turned to a disturbance in the crowd. A young man bounced up and down about two rows away from the teacher. He was shouting inarticulately, and I assumed that he was excitedly praising God. But the teacher ended this assumption when he pointed at the young man and spoke sharply. 'Stop that! Come out of him.'

"As suddenly as his bouncing ecstasy started, the young man disappeared into the tight press of people. Though he might not have actually fallen to the ground, he completely ceased his frenetic noise and movement.

"The teacher didn't pursue him; rather, he touched and healed a small boy held by the lean, tan arms of a man who must have been his father. The little boy had a twisted foot, turned about forty-five degrees inward. When the teacher touched him, the foot thrashed on its own accord, quite unnaturally. After a few seconds, the thrashing stopped and the foot looked perfectly straight.

"The teacher touched a man on the forehead who had a severely smashed nose. When the teacher's hand came off of the man's forehead, the man grabbed his nose with both hands and shouted in surprise. When he removed his hands, his nose stood straight and unmarred. He smiled as he inhaled vigorously through his restored nose.

"People who had been healed pushed their way through the crowd, away from where the teacher stood surrounded by his friends. Thousands of people remained on that hill, but many of them had moved out of the press of people. Some were setting up camp for the night, away from the center of activity.

"A small group of young men had gathered at the front of the mob-like crowd and were reaching out to the teacher. He took hold of one young man's hand and shouted to the others to take their friend's hand. They each turned to the next and all of them stood linked together. An older man standing near the end of this line attached himself to the last young man, clearly guessing what the teacher intended.

"The teacher made no sign of greater effort; he simply stood still a moment and hung on to the first young man, who started to vibrate. His friend next to him started to bob up and down and the next one to jerk back and forth, and so on down the line. The young man who had created a distraction a few minutes before was part of this healing chain. The older man who had tagged on to the end of the group of youngsters shouted joyously, holding up his hand. He waved it and flexed it freely.

"The teacher released the first young man, who stood still, staring and speechless, tears running down his face. All of the young men slowly gathered together and turned to push away from the teacher now. Some of them, at least, would certainly need to find a place to sit down and absorb whatever it was that they had just experienced.

"Others filled in at the front, reaching for the teacher like he was a celebrity they wanted to touch. The teacher responded by touching each of those hands extended to him, some very briefly, and some holding on a bit longer. The recipients would react in a wide variety of ways as they recovered from sicknesses or injuries that I couldn't know about.

"The teacher's attention turned to his friends, a concerned look creasing his brow as I had seldom seen all that day. I could see from their slumped shoulders and growing sweat stains that the press of people constantly leaning in toward him had begun to sap their strength. The efforts that protected him from the weight of those desperate people wore on Peter, John and the others. The teacher directed Peter toward a large flat rock, where he could sit and his friends could more easily control the crowd.

"They moved like a phalanx of Roman soldiers, together as one person, gaining strength from one another. As they moved, the teacher briefly touched each of his friends, perhaps to bless them with strength for their work.

"When they reached the rock, the crowd's push had slackened enough so that the bodyguards could arrange themselves in front of and behind the teacher, without having to lock arms to protect him. The edges of the rock provided space, and sitting on the rock allowed the teacher some much-needed rest. By this time, he had been healing people for at least ten hours, with little respite. He showed no sign, however, that he would stop before the sun went down."

When Walter stopped, I felt more than ever that I didn't want to leave the story, to return from that faraway place and time.

"James, you look as if your body is present but your soul is somewhere else."

I snickered, remembering him telling of a Native American belief that when a person traveled he had to stop occasionally to allow his soul to catch up with him. I certainly felt like that traveler when I followed Walter through those vivid and compelling dreams.

When I tried to speak I couldn't keep my voice from cracking as my throat tightened with the longing. "I want it to be true." That was all I could manage.

Jillian chimed in. "I know what you mean." Her voice sounded as choked as mine. She took a deep breath and sniffled a bit.

Walter smiled and nodded ever so slightly. "I think that's the starting place for faith. You have to want it."

I thought about that. Somehow the word *faith* didn't fit the yearning I felt.

I spoke, my voice a bit more under my control. "I don't know if that's it, but I'm finding this whole experience completely destabilizing." I paused, gathering my thoughts. "I guess the cognitive dissonance comes from the power of something that I can't see or verify. How could your retelling of your dream have so much impact on me?"

Walter looked at me with what I always thought of as his sly fox look, his eyes squinted as if assessing me even as he grinned. "Maybe it's because they're not my dreams but really your dreams. I'm just the messenger."

I had no answer for that, and didn't even try.

He strained to stifle a yawn and covered his mouth with one hand.

Jillian broke into my mental wandering. "It looks like the professor could use a nap before dinner."

Not only had I noticed how tired Walter looked before the dream narration, but it had been a long story. I had also forgotten my dinner and concert plans with Jillian. When I looked at her, it seemed as if her body was poised to jump out of the bed, a brief look telling me she was ready to go eat.

"Yes, that does sound good," Walter said. "Would you mind asking the nurses to hold my dinner? I'm much more tired than hungry tonight."

Jillian and I agreed. We each hugged Walter as he got up to move to his bed. We said good night, though it wasn't even five o'clock yet. It seemed most likely that he would sleep for the night, judging by the angle of his eyelids and his languid rise from the chair.

As we walked to the car, I wondered aloud if the excitement of the dreams was taking a toll on Walter.

Jillian offered a low and measured response. "At eighty-seven, he could fully recover from the stroke and still pass away quietly."

Here came another strange disconnect for me. Why bother healing him if he's not going to live much longer? I decided not to say this to Jillian, feeling that I too often played the role of doubting Thomas, or even devil's advocate.

Instead, I kissed her on the cheek and opened the car door for her.

I could tell from her playful smile that she favored this response over another spin of faithless questions from me.

Chapter Thirteen
The Setting Sun

The Saturday concert followed by Sunday church reminded me of my high school days, when most of my activities rotated through my church youth group. It had been a long time since I'd felt so connected to church and especially to what was going on there. In fact, it occurred to me that I had perhaps never owned the central truths of my faith more firmly than I did that Sunday morning.

As we sang a song about the power of Jesus's resurrection I had to take a few deep breaths to keep from dissolving into tears. Jillian looked at me, her strong, sweet alto voice turning toward my welcoming ear. New self-consciousness, promoted by that look from her, helped me to stifle the threatening emotional outburst. This was not one of *those* churches, after all. Was I becoming one of *those* Christians? That thought, a fear of emotionalism perhaps, poked and badgered me into distraction through the rest of the morning. When I forced myself to focus on the words of the preacher, inevitably some profound truth would arrow into my heart and I would spiral back to fighting to restrain my feelings.

At lunch, after church, Jillian made a comment that seemed a sideways approach to my church service struggles. "Sometimes I get this urge to run out of the worship service, to find a private place where I can really let loose what I'm feeling about something in a song or the sermon."

I hadn't notice her wrestling with unbridled emotions during the service, and I think of myself as fairly perceptive. This led me to assume she was offering a polite opening for me to talk about what I was feeling. A sneaky therapist trick if ever I saw one.

As I laughed I had to cover my mouth to keep from showing too much salad to the off-duty shrink across the table.

"Not too subtle, huh?"

I shook my head, swallowed my bite of salad, and drank some water. "Not *too* subtle," I agreed. "Just subtle enough."

I watched as she picked through her salad and glanced up at me. "Yeah, I was feeling like that today," I said, "only, running for a place to let loose never crossed my mind, emotional repression comes more naturally."

Jillian just acknowledged my self-evaluation with one small sound and no comment. She seemed to sense my discomfort with pursing the topic further.

We had arranged to spend the rest of the day with Walter at my house, hoping to give him some time away from the nursing home's institutional setting. Finishing our meal, I paid the check after a bantering tussle with Jillian, involving questions of economic equality and the place of women in human history. I was proud of myself for holding my ground, male chauvinist or otherwise.

The weather forecast had prompted my idea of getting Walter out of the home, a balmy forty-five degrees with occasional sunshine accompanied us from the restaurant to Walter's place. I had last spoken with him that morning over the phone, catching him crunching toast for breakfast. For supper, I planned to warm some lasagna I had made a couple of weeks ago and stowed in the freezer.

Stable on two legs with only a perfunctory cane, Walter was much easier to help in and out of the car than the last time we accompanied him into the wider world. Though he seemed jovial all along the way, he gave me the impression of a man trying to look stronger than he was. His skin seemed translucent to me, his eyes slightly more sunken, and I heard him huffing and puffing after the slightest exertion. I looked at him in the rear view mirror at one stop light, a dark green fedora on his head and his glasses slipping down his nose again. I was glad we had arranged to spend the day with him.

Settled into my living room, he sat with his feet up in my leather recliner and a cup of Constant Comment tea at his elbow. I kept it in the house just for Walter, though it had been many months since he had been there.

After holding the surprise for us through the entire transition from his place to mine, he cleared his throat. "I had another dream last night."

I had been wondering what the three of us should do that afternoon. Now I had at least a partial answer.

Jillian encouraged him. "Well, if you feel up to it, I would certainly love to hear you tell about it."

I raised my eyebrows. "You'd better check out her fees before you agree to that."

They both gave me nearly identical scolding looks, so I pretended to be more serious.

"Yes, please go ahead, don't mind me."

Walter laughed huskily, took a sip of tea, and cleared his throat again.

"It was both inspiring and painful to see the teacher barely able to sit up due to exhaustion, yet still attending to the needs of the sick or injured. I wondered, as I saw his condition, whether what followed was an attempt to take advantage of that weariness.

"A woman who looked to be in her forties, wearing a dark red head covering and a long black robe, approached. A group of two dozen or so younger men and women accompanied her. She bowed before the teacher, who sat with John on one side and James on the other.

"'Why have you come?' the teacher said bluntly, an unusual greeting in the context of that day of gracious giving and merciful healing.

"'You know, don't you?' The woman replied with a sarcastic bend in her voice. She lured and repulsed me at the same time,

And He Healed Them All

with a sort of unisex beauty and intangible magnetism.

"The teacher answered. 'You are sick, and you cannot heal yourself, nor have your disciples succeeded in healing you. So you come to me as a last resort . . . and as a challenge.'

"The mysterious woman yielded to a harsh coughing fit as if to confirm his diagnosis, and then smirked when she had finished. 'A challenge? How can anything be a challenge to you?' Her voice dripped with irony.

"The teacher ignored her question and asked one of his own. 'Do you come to me to be freed from *more* than your sickness?'

"'Hmm. Is that what I should expect from you?'

"'You know how I feel about your craft and the source of your powers.'

"'Yes, you think that because your Father created this power you can keep it from the rest of us. But I also know that you heal all who come to you for help, without conditions. You haven't turned away anyone.'

"'No, I haven't turned anyone away.' He sighed heavily, as if his weariness verified this.

"He signaled her to come closer. She hesitated. For a moment it looked as if she might turn and run. Her torso wavered backward and forward, as if caught between two powerful forces, like a small metal ball at the mercy of two great magnets. The force with greater gravity prevailed. She lurched forward and dropped to the ground with a shriek. Instantly, all of her followers fell to the ground as well, some stumbling as they tried to turn and flee.

"The witch, for that's what she was, writhed and twisted, alternately shrieking and muttering in some unrecognizable language.

The teacher commanded in a low stern voice. '"Be quiet!'

"The muttering stopped, but the shrieking increased. He seemed to mind that less.

"'Release her, now,' he said, with force.

"At this the witch stopped, as if knocked unconscious, but two of her followers took up the writhing and shrieking in an eerily identical fashion.

"'Stop that,' the teacher insisted. At this, all of them began to shake and mutter and shriek as if in waves, from one side to the other, then from the front to the back. The crowd pressed back, away from the mêlée, some even flopping to the ground, seized by the same gyrations and wailing.

"The teacher slid off of the rock onto the ground between Peter and Andrew, who stood in front of him. He crouched and pressed both hands to the ground, as if seizing the earth beneath him. He closed his eyes and began to recite, 'Hear, O Israel: the Lord Our God, the Lord is One God.' He never raised his voice. 'Hear, O Israel: the Lord Our God, the Lord is One God.' He spoke with determination and confidence. With his hands planted on the earth, he worshipped the one who had spun the planet into space.

"The confusion and noise began to dissipate as he repeated that confession, known as *The Shema*. The teacher's helpers began to attend to the people who had not come with the witch but had fallen to the ground with her acolytes. His disciples raised these startled men and women to their feet, even rebuking spirits they had perhaps brought with them.

"The teacher looked at the witch. Their eyes met and they began to crawl toward each other, eliminating the few feet that separated them. The teacher remained sedate and stern, as did the witch. Their eyes neither wandered nor blinked.

"The witch did not mutter, did not shriek; she did not show any signs of the insanity that had controlled her just moments before. She seemed to be herself, but it was not a contrite and submissive self, her chin still held high and her eyes glaring. Nevertheless, the teacher rose to his knees and grasped her face with both hands, breathing a single long breath into her nose and mouth.

"The witch inhaled, as if receiving a healing vapor into her ailing lungs. She closed her eyes and exhaled. No coughing ensued. She smiled, and, for the first time, she looked like someone I wouldn't mind meeting in the real world, a pleasant look in her eyes.

"The teacher's friends assisted the witch's followers to their feet. As each of her underlings regained control of themselves, they turned their attention on their leader. They watched her, while vigilantly casting glances at the teacher and his followers, looking like they wanted to escape, but uncertain which way led to safety.

"Peter and James helped the teacher to his feet and back to the rock.

"The witch stood up with the help of two of her followers. She brushed herself off and straightened her gowns and jewelry, a few bits of which had to be retrieved from the ground. For a moment she stood still, examining one particular amulet, which looked as if it had been melted in a fire. The pure gold trinket apparently maintained only a rough remnant of its former shape. She showed no anger over this destruction but seemed fascinated by the phenomenon.

"As she gathered her wits about her, the witch's followers gravitated toward her. The rest of the crowd shuffled forward to close in around them, trying to approach the teacher without getting too close to them.

"When I last saw the witch, she and her acolytes were pushing through the crowd under the dim light of early evening. I don't know all of what had happened to her. It seemed an unfinished story. Part of healing everyone who came certainly allowed that the gift of health meant different things to different people. I could see the possibility of someone like the witch being healed of her physical ailment without following that sign to repentance from her way of life.

"The teacher rested in his place on the rock. A woman and a boy, who seemed to be her son, approached the teacher, guided by his friends. The boy lifted a bandaged hand to the teacher. I spotted a jagged, half-healed cut on his cheek as well. The teacher looked at him then gently touched his face. As if by an invisible eraser, the cut on his face faded completely. The boy, about nine years old, put his injured hand up to his face. Then he tugged at the bandage to remove it. His mother moved to stop him, perhaps out of motherly habit, but then checked herself and let her son reveal the perfectly healthy hand beneath the blood-stained bandage.

"The boy raised his eyebrows and looked at the teacher, who smiled at him. The boy returned the smile, looked up at his mother, and then followed her off to the side.

"In the next minute, the teacher healed a woman complaining of stomach pain, a man hunched under back pain, a small girl who was partially blind, and a boy walking with crutches. With one word or one gentle touch, each of them left their ailment behind and walked away healthy and strong, smiling, laughing and praising God.

"I noticed then a boy, about eight years old, standing off to the side. He wasn't advancing toward the teacher but watched the proceedings from where he stood. Behind the boy stood a man, I suppose it was his father, occasionally asking the boy a question. The boy would offer an explanation or nod his head. As I watched the boy's reaction to the continuous stream of people being healed, it seemed to me that he was not watching the teacher nor the people who came sick and left well; rather, he was watching something taking place around the teacher, something that I apparently couldn't see.

"An elderly rabbi hobbled before the teacher, bowed slightly, and then jumped half a foot off the ground. He dropped his walking stick, which clattered to the stony ground just before the rabbi himself landed nimbly on two feet. Instead of that waddle I have seen on people needing a hip replacement he walked straight and vigorously.

"Behind the rabbi, at the angle from which I was watching, that little boy clapped his hands and pointed at the air above the rejoicing man. He laughed a joyous, childish giggle at the sight that only he seemed to see. This side commotion caught the attention of the teacher. He followed the boy's gaze to the air above the rabbi, and then waved the boy to come to him.

"The boy smiled but shyly avoided eye contact. He tugged his father's hand, and then stepped to the teacher's side. The teacher asked his name.

"'I am Simeon. And this is my father, Ezekiel.'

"The teacher put his hand on Simeon's shoulder. 'What are you watching, my boy?'

"Simeon studied the teacher, as if to measure what sort of question that was. 'The angels,' he said.

"The teacher gave a lopsided smile and drew Simeon close to him. He spoke into the boy's ear. The teacher seemed to be explaining things, for he pointed and then spoke to Simeon; he gestured, and the boy laughed. Then the conversation appeared to take a serious turn, and the teacher pulled Simeon a bit closer. The teacher leaned forward and spoke softly, so all I could hear was an instructive and cautionary tone in his voice. The boy focused on the teacher's kind face, as if he longed to capture every movement of that face, as much as every word spoken to him.

"When he finished, the teacher said, 'Do you understand?'

"'Yes, teacher,' said Simeon. And his father nodded as well, for he had been close enough to understand what the teacher had told his son.

"I could see various people looking around at the air above them and above the teacher, probably trying to see what Simeon saw. More than a few of the teacher's friends joined in this search, though most of them did so surreptitiously. Simeon and his father moved off to the side, I didn't see them again after that.

"Four small girls approached the teacher, accompanied by a pair of women who may have been a mother and grandmother. The teacher didn't wait for any explanation before he passed his hand over the four girls, who toppled like dry grass in a sudden wind. From their landing place on the ground, all four began speaking at once, predicting what was going to happen to the teacher, what would happen to each of his disciples, and what would happen to their mother and grandmother. They spoke of the glory of God and the proceedings in heaven at that very moment. They spoke of the fall of the nation of Israel and the rise of the Gentiles to receive the grace of God. All speaking at once in cacophony, I managed to pick out mere strands of their foresight.

"What their ailments had been, I never knew. Regardless, the mother and grandmother seemed overjoyed to hear their little ones prophesying. They stood over the girls, who lay with arms and legs sprawled across each other—yet perfectly comfortable it seemed.

"The teacher turned his attention to a young woman who approached with another woman, who appeared to her sister. The first woman seemed to be both deaf and blind and fairly difficult for her sister to control. She flailed about and recoiled spasmodically in response to any physical touch, intentional or otherwise. In that condition, a full day in that crowd must have been truly traumatic.

"The teacher paused before stating his command. 'Deaf and blind spirit, be gone!'

"The afflicted woman grabbed at her head as if in great pain, holding her hands over both ears. Her eyes flew wide open and she began to look around, apparently focusing on people as if seeing them clearly. Then she began to twist back and forth and to shriek while still holding her hands over her ears. Her screeching caused others to clap their hands over their ears as well. I wasn't sure what was happening—was the gift of sudden sight and sound too much for her to take in?

"The teacher hauled himself off the rock and put his hand on her head. Immediately she calmed, dropped her hands to her side, and gazed at the teacher's face. She seemed suddenly enraptured with him, no longer tortured by the sights and sounds that assailed her, but focused on one thing, one person. As the teacher watched, her sister took her hand and put it on her own face. The healed woman closed her eyes, as if she could only recognize the other woman without sight. The two women embraced, united in tears and harmonizing with the sister speaking words of relief while the healed woman added inarticulate sounds of joy.

"Returning to his seat on the rock, the teacher's obviously weary frame folded onto the restful refuge. A few of his industrious helpers busied themselves with building a back and an armrest for him to lean on. No doubt this was a project that the former carpenter could appreciate: the selection of the best stones and their careful placement to serve the intended purpose. Others of his friends kept the people coming to him, directing them around the two women still locked in an embrace and the four girls lying on the ground prophesying.

"While his helpers modified his seating, the crowd slacked their forward press. One man, however, took advantage of the lull and slipped in front of the teacher.

"'What do you want?' the teacher said, his near monotone indicating his weariness.

"The man opened his shirt, exposing a festering sore near his breast bone. "I have these sores all over me.' He pulled up the hem of his garment to show a smaller sore on his calf.

"The teacher beckoned the man closer. 'Let me see that one on your chest again.' At the same time he scooped a small handful of dust off of the rock. When the man showed the sore, the teacher held open his hand and blew the dust onto the sore.

"When the man instinctively brushed the dust off of his exposed chest, the sore disappeared with the dust. He looked further down inside his shirt, where other sores must have been. He pushed up his sleeves, but I saw no sores. Then he looked at his leg. 'They're gone!' He laughed. 'They're all gone!' And several people praised God in response as the young man thanked the teacher and pushed back into the crowd.

"Those who remained, pushed forward. Peter, Andrew, and Bartholomew pressed back, positioning themselves directly in front of the teacher. He lifted his feet up beside him to keep them from being crushed against the front of the rock. He leaned on the armrest his friends had built. Many of the people who pressed against the three men could reach the teacher still. He obliged by touching any hand presented to him.

"A woman with a misshapen face looked over the arms of the bodyguards so the teacher could see her. Her face was nearly flat on one side and rounded on the other. The distortion to her nose most likely hindered her breathing, but I wonder if that motivated her as much as a natural longing for beauty. The teacher leaned forward and cupped her face in both hands. When he let go, her head shook rapidly, throwing her to the ground. The people around her lifted the small woman above the crush and passed her limp body to the teacher's friends waiting on one side, where two of the women received her and found a place to lay her. Those women, along with me, were the first to see the new and improved face the woman had received.

"The teacher continued to touch heads and hands in rapid succession. Many of those healed tried to leave, shoving through the dense mob. But swimming against the forward press overcame many, and they lost their balance, though they couldn't properly fall to the ground. Again, strong arms lifted some of the smaller people up to the top of the crowd and passed them from hand to hand to a less heavily packed part of the hillside. I thought that this must be similar to the mosh pit at a rock concert. The process of people stopping to help move the previous supplicants out of the way before reaching the teacher lessened the forward pressure somewhat. James and John repeatedly waded into the crowd to make sure that no one was trampled. These were rough, work-hardened men, but they displayed a measure of gentleness, even for crowd control, in the service of the teacher.

"The teacher touched babies and small children held up by half a dozen parents, who appeared to have banded together and pushed through the crowd as one. One baby girl with a withered arm, barely half the size of the other, hung suspended over Peter and Bartholomew, held in strong hands. The teacher touched the little girl and her withered arm immediately grew to match the other. Because of the intense press of people, few enjoyed the sight of that little arm expanding to normal size.

"In this context—failing light, the teacher's growing weariness, the crowd pressing in on him—I suddenly feared for the teacher's life. Without warning, it entered my mind that the remarkable healing of the baby's arm was not the only thing that would be undetected in that throng. Then I noticed a tall man with a long, jet-black beard, who was wedged in among the broad variety of people seeking the teacher.

"As I focused on this man, I noticed that he made eye contact with two of the teacher's followers, Judas Iscariot and Simon the Zealot. As I reflected on the dream later, I thought of what I had learned long ago, in graduate school, about a group of patriots known as the Sicari, Jewish nationalist assassins who used the cover of a large crowd to dispatch Romans and Roman collaborators. I caught a small movement of the stranger's hand as he adjusted something hidden up one sleeve and then another under his belt. My attention was drawn to these movements, as if I was supposed to understand who this man was.

"The teacher's bodyguards kept their master from being crushed by an enthusiastic crowd, but would they be able to protect him against assassination attempts? I thought too of what scholars have said regarding Judas and Simon's possible association with those rebels and assassins, and I wondered about their eye contact with this ominous stranger.

"Even as the assassin neared the front of the crowd, Judas and Simon moved stealthily toward the teacher. I realized then that, from where they stood, they could see people before they reached the teacher, watching perhaps for just such a threat as this man.

"Judas reached Andrew just before the assassin did. Simon managed to make eye-contact with Bartholomew, who was directly in front of the teacher, and thus Bartholomew was alerted to some threat just as the assassin reached out his hand among the many hands stretched toward the teacher. Simon, Bartholomew, and Judas rushed into the crowd and attempted to seize him.

"Peter was the lone remaining bodyguard between the teacher and the crowd. Andrew had followed Judas, Simon, and Bartholomew once he saw their target. The task of holding back the crowd, however, became easier after the defenders rushed the assassin. The front line of the crowd collapsed backward when the four men lunged in. The guards knocked the armed man to the ground and Judas and Simon each held one of his hands.

They also each seized one of his concealed daggers.

"The disciples apparently discovered that the assassin's hands were empty, his hidden daggers having to be retrieved from their sheaths. And they must have realized that they had not thwarted an assassination attempt, as they assumed.

"'Simon, Judas, let him up.' The teacher shouted above the din.

"The two men, holding the daggers, released their captive. Andrew and Bartholomew kept their grip on the stranger, but did so to help him up off the ground. The sight of the five disheveled, dusty and sweaty men—two of them holding weapons—shocked the surrounding crowd into silence.

"The teacher took command of the situation. 'Bring him to me.'

"The crowd moved back, allowing the assassin and his escort room, though Peter stood between the assassin and the teacher. I had seen Peter hit at least one man that day already, and I could see his fists clenched again.

"'It's all right, Peter. You can step aside,' the teacher said. To the assassin, he said, 'You're not sleeping at night.'

"The sad looking man put his hand on his stomach. 'My stomach bothers me most nights, and I can't get much sleep.' His voice was plaintive and mellow.

"The teacher leaned forward and put his hand in the middle of the man's chest. The man moaned and drew his shoulders up. Then he relaxed and let out a heavy sigh. He wavered slightly before righting himself. Thanking the teacher, he backed into the crowd, who opened up to let him pass, then closed the gap, swallowing him up.

"The sudden violence underscored the extent to which the teacher was sacrificing himself for the people during this long day of intense emotions and physical strains. This latest event seemed to settle the crowd's previous frenzied push. In spite of the approaching night and many still hoping for healing, the crowd let up their press to reach the teacher that night. Perhaps they could tell that he wasn't going anywhere."

Walter told us about this dream in two parts, the second part after dinner. I had stoked a fire in the fireplace and the lasagna sat heavy in our stomachs, topped off with a chocolate cake that Jillian brought over. With all that, and telling the second half of the dream, Walter had begun to sink into the recliner, surrendering to the warmth and weariness of the evening.

In the brief silence after Walter had finished, Jillian sniffled. I looked in time to see her swipe at a tear. She smiled at me, perhaps remembering our conversation that morning about my suppressed emotions.

"Obviously, these dreams have become very real to me," she said with a little laugh. She dabbed her nose with a tissue. "I feel the teacher's openness to everyone, his desire to touch and heal everyone. In my mind this seems right, just like I would expect, but it's reaching something deep inside me. I guess I'm riding on the realization that if he loved all of them, then it must be true that he loves me too."

My instant thought was, "How could he not love you?" But I held that back, allowing myself to absorb her explanation instead.

Walter laughed a churlish laugh that I would almost call a giggle. I looked sharply at him to try to figure out what he was doing. He sensed the apparent impropriety and apologized.

"I'm popping my cork over here, trying to contain what I came to realize earlier today, as I prayed about the significance of the dreams. They're not just for me, as I've said. But they're not just for James either." He looked directly at Jillian when he said this, though he barely moved his head, so comfortably ensconced in the voluminous chair.

After a few seconds of silence, I addressed practical considerations. "I think it's time to get you back to your place."

Walter's head rolled from side to side as if it floated there above his resting body. "Wish I still had that wheelchair," he said. "This thing doesn't have wheels on it does it?"

We both laughed with him and helped him slowly rise out of the chair, once we pushed the footrest back down to the floor.

Taking him back home that night, we continued to talk, Walter's aged baritone massaging our hearts and minds out of the darkness in the backseat.

Even so, my mind tripped back a few months to the urgent call I'd received from the hospital, telling me of Walter's stroke. I remembered the nighttime drive to the emergency room. And I recalled how little like Walter that inert old man in the hospital bed seemed.

On this night, five months after his stroke, Walter was as peaceful and affable as I had ever known him to be. I smiled at the irony that now too I found it hard to recognize the moderate intellectual who had mentored me through college and the early stages of my teaching career. The mystical dreamer that had replaced that old Walter left me quietly amused, and deeply uncomfortable.

Chapter Fourteen
At the End of the Day

On Tuesday afternoon, I called Walter and found that he hadn't yet had another dream. Jillian had invited me to come with her to meet her mother and help with some small chores around her mother's apartment. I arranged to see Walter the next day, whether he had a dream that night or not. It's funny how we had come to expect the next dream, like a new episode on TV. I guess we had been conditioned by their regularity, coming every couple of days.

Meanwhile, I welcomed the chance to see another side of Jillian. Beyond the obvious opportunity to meet her mother, and perhaps to see something of Jillian's future, I was interested to learn how she treated the woman who had raised her, but who now depended very heavily on her.

We ate a quick dinner together after work. Her mother would have liked to have cooked for us, but a severe fall and a failed hip replacement had limited her mobility. She also had dietary restrictions that made sharing a meal too complicated for my first meeting with her. At least, this is what Jillian had concluded. I was learning that she liked to keep things simple, a refreshing contrast to my own tendency to get tangled up in complications of my own devising.

Jillian's mother, Carol, lived in a fairly new apartment building with heavily padded carpets in the hallways, which seemed to suck sound right out of the air. The first word I spoke seemed to stop dead, six inches from my mouth. Somehow this inspired me to lower my voice still more.

Jillian led the way to the plain wooden door with number 406 on it, opening it with a key on her key ring, sparing her mother the walk to greet us there.

She called out as soon as she opened the door. "Hello, Mother." Somehow it felt as if her voice could carry more than a couple of feet inside the apartment. We could certainly hear *Wheel of Fortune* on TV from where we entered.

"Hello, Dear." Her mother's slightly shrill voice floated from the other room. I could tell from the sound of the last word, that she was starting to get up to meet us.

"No need to get up, Mom. We can come and see you where you're sitting." We had passed through the narrow hallway to the living room, where and I looked over Jillian's shoulder at a woman in her late seventies slowly rocking left and right in her seat, gradually scooting forward so she could stand. Jillian handed me the storage container of soup she had been carrying so she could catch her mother.

"It's okay," she started to say, trying to correct her mother gently.

But Carol said, "Well, I want to greet your guest properly, don't I?" She sounded slightly contentious, though perhaps not genuinely perturbed, as she insisted on doing things her own way.

Instead of resisting, Jillian helped her mother to stand. "Okay, Mother. I understand."

With a full open smile, Carol Moore greeted me. "Oh, James I'm so glad to meet you." She offered her right hand as Jillian supported her left arm.

I took her hand in mine and leaned forward to kiss her on the cheek.

"Oh, my, yes." Her smile turned sweeter, like a girl pleasantly surprised.

"Mrs. Moore, such a pleasure to meet you," I said, still holding her hand.

Carol stood at least six inches shorter than Jillian, I guessed that not all of that difference could be accounted for by aging and a bad hip replacement. Apparently Jillian had inherited her height from her father. But her mother's face clearly looked like a projection of Jillian in thirty years or more. Paler, grayer skin, with wrinkles around the eyes, and puffiness in her cheeks masked Jillian's beauty, which had certainly once been Carol's.

"So you teach philosophy?"

"Yes, that's right."

"Not much else you can do with that besides teach, huh?" she said, as Jillian shepherded her back to her recliner.

I laughed. "Not much."

"So what would you do if you didn't teach?"

"Well, I like to work with my hands. I've fixed up my old house on my own, and I've imagined doing that for a living."

"Oh, really? How did you get into that?" She scooted back into her seat as Jillian took the container of soup to the kitchen, smiling at me out of her mother's view. It wasn't quite an apologetic smile, maybe sort of a "Welcome to my world" kind of smile.

"I worked for my dad's construction company in high school and during the summers in college. I learned about carpentry then."

"Oh, that's nice, and so handy to know, isn't it?"

By this point I noted that each sentence ended in a question mark, and I wondered how to turn the conversation. Jillian returned from the kitchen and bailed me out.

"Mom, you've used up quite a few of your twenty questions already, you might want to save some for later."

Her mother shrugged. "Just getting to know James. There's nothing wrong with being curious, is there?"

I smiled at Jillian. "Does that one count?"

Jillian caught my joke, but Carol missed it, so I settled down, not wanting to bypass her in the conversation.

In all, I'm sure she asked more than twenty questions, and I asked a few of my own. We did get to know each other pretty well for one evening. Carol insisted that I eat nearly a whole plate of chocolate chip cookies, a bigger sugar infusion than I would normally have taken, but well worth the sacrifice.

When it came time to leave, and Carol again insisted on exercising her painful hips by standing up to say good-bye, I gave her a big hug.

"It was grand to meet you, Carol." I addressed her as she had requested, by her first name, in hopes of preserving a measure of youth, I suppose.

"Oh, you were good to come see me and put up with all my questions." She glanced sideways at Jillian with her head bent slightly.

"Don't worry about the questions. How else are you going to find out what you want to know?" I said.

Jillian and I left together to ride back to my place in her car. A work night for both of us we said goodnight and parted on the driveway, the moderate day reverting to piercing cold under an occasional clear patch in the clouds. We agreed to talk on the phone the next day.

In fact, I called Jillian that next afternoon after talking to Walter. For the first time he actively urged me to visit in order to hear his latest dream.

"I really want you and Jillian to both be here tonight, if you can. It would mean a lot to me," he said over the phone.

That was far more ardent than any of his previous invitations, and from it I gathered that this was a particularly significant dream. I wondered if this might be the last one. The story had progressed to the latter stages of that day in Jesus's life, and it felt to us that the dreams would not continue beyond the close of the day.

As it turned out I was right.

***

"I wanted you both here because this is the last one," Walter said.

Jillian and I absorbed the news.

Walter narrated this last dream sitting in his favorite chair, as usual. His growing belief that receiving and passing on these dreams represented his life's final purpose seemed to add a bit of formality to his tone. Jillian and I sat in our usual places that late February evening and listened to Walter tell us his last dream.

"The day had faded, the sky darkening from light to medium to dark blue. The sun left a thin stain of red and gold along the horizon. People started campfires on the hillside and rolled out bedding. A few even setup tents. Others assembled makeshift shelters out of whatever they had with them.

"Many who had been healed that day had not remained; therefore, the crowd had thinned somewhat. Others stayed, although the teacher had already touched them. Thousands more waited to receive healing or to assist someone they had brought to the teacher. New people arrived every hour, as word continued to spread around the countryside that the teacher from Nazareth was on this hill next to the lake.

"The teacher sat on the flat rock, leaning on the makeshift armrest and relying on Peter and John to help keep him steady. Others of his followers served him water and bites of food. In this condition, the manner of the healing had changed. The teacher sat in one place and people walked or were carried past him.

"He conserved his movements, nodding to some, saying simply a word to others. Occasionally he instructed those around him to hold people up so that he could touch them, or he asked his followers to touch someone in his stead, so that many of the healings came without the teacher's direct touch.

"I recalled the many people he had embraced that day, how many electric connections he had made, as people writhed or collapsed or simply vibrated while he held on to them. I imagined how many times he had knelt and stood back up. He often forcefully seized or even struck people. All of this added up to natural physical exhaustion. But what about the spiritual effort he had exerted? What about the toll of all of those confrontations with unearthly voices, the authoritative commands, and the imposition of his will against those unseen enemies?

"In spite of this extreme weariness, he continued to lean into his work, to address the needs of the crowd that continued to stream to him for help.

"I saw a woman standing before the teacher, holding a little boy who must have been her son. I could see deep grief written in her sunken eyes and grimacing lips. The boy's head bandaged with an old stained cloth, I saw no sign of life in that little body. The teacher leaned forward and the mother moved her boy closer.

"The teacher touched two fingers to the boy's forehead. When the boy suddenly moved, the mother nearly dropped him, uttering a little cry. The boy came to life, arms and legs moving, his head rising to look at his dark surroundings, just like any healthy child waking. John stepped up and helped the mother lower the boy to stand on his own, ruffling his hair, now free from the bandage. The boy looked as if he were trying to decide what kind of dream he was having while the mother shuffled him away, staying as close as she could.

"A tall thin man standing near the teacher allowed another mother to move past him to present her child, this one a little girl, who looked less than three years old. The teacher touched the girl's head. Her little eyes followed his hand as if it moved of its own will and she had no way to control it or what came from it. In the moment that he touched her, her mouth popped open in surprise and she made an inarticulate noise, like someone who had never learned to speak. More deaf ears healed it seemed.

"Again I watched that tall man let someone pass him, this time a woman leading an old man with a severe limp. Apparently the tall man was yielding to those with more pressing needs than he had. As the sun disappeared and darkness arrived, I couldn't help but think that the people must have known that the teacher would stop healing soon, and this man risked missing his healing that night, by assuring that others received theirs.

"I noticed the teacher glance at the tall thin man as he allowed another person to move ahead of him. 'You, what is your name?'

"The man raised his eyebrows, clearly surprised that the teacher addressed him. 'I am Able, son of Issachar.'

"'Able, son of Issachar, you are healed. Go and be blessed all the days of your life.'

"Able responded with a look that seemed to say, 'that settles it for me,' as if there were no question that what the teacher said was so. He thanked the teacher and yielded his place to another. As he pushed through the crowd, I could see him gingerly turn his head left and then right. He stopped and explored his full range of movement. The teacher had apparently healed his neck in some way.

"Those in need kept moving toward the teacher's seat on the rock, though the increasing darkness made it more difficult to see. A man with his elbow locked at a ninety-degree angle walked away hinging his arm up and down, a large smile on his face. A woman who approached holding her lower abdomen stretched herself and smiled when she felt her healing completed. A mother and father carrying a boy with a misshapen leg, perhaps broken and not set properly, placed him before the teacher and then chased after him when he sped off to jump and celebrate.

"After several more such healings, the teacher merely waved his hand over, or even just motioned with his head toward the sick and injured.

"A woman, who had been watching the teacher's weary efforts as she waited to bring two small boys before him, spoke to Peter. 'If we could just touch the hem of the teacher's robe, we could all be healed. He needn't do anything but just sit there, don't you think?'

"Peter stared blankly at the woman for a few seconds, either because her idea seemed far-fetched, or because he couldn't explain why they hadn't already thought of this. Peter didn't have to answer the suggestion, however. The teacher had overheard. 'Yes, Mother, that would be fine.'

"He instructed James and Andrew to lead the people to him, so that they could touch his sleeve or the hem of his robe.

"He accepted a blanket as a cushion beneath him, and leaned back against a second blanket to soften his stone couch. He laid his hands on his lap so that his sleeves were easy to reach, as was the hem of his robe. He watched the people coming and going in turn. At times two or even three would touch him at once. It obviously pleased him to give them freedom from pain or restriction or weakness, for he smiled and occasionally chuckled.

"People on stretchers and mats were carried past his feet where they could touch his robe. Some needed assistance from those who carried them. One old man couldn't move at all, so a young man, who may have been his son, took hold of the old man's hand and gently raised it to brush the teacher's robe. Instantly, the man's hand shot up, throwing the younger man back as he lost his grip. The old man sat up, looked from his son to the teacher. 'You . . . you were in my dream.'

"The teacher tipped his head and smiled weakly. Perhaps he had been in that dream and was fully aware of it. As the young man and the other stretcher bearer gathered the bedding, the old man stretched his legs and shook hands with James, Andrew, and Peter. As they walked away into the dusk, I heard the man ask, 'What day is this?' And I heard the son trying to explain.

"Most of the people touched his sleeve as they passed the teacher, moving from his right to his left. A woman with some disease that had caused her arm to swell grotesquely touched that almost inhuman arm to the teacher's sleeve. Her hand surged ahead of her, as if yanked by an invisible force. She grabbed the swollen hand with her good one. When she did, I saw the swelling disappear in a matter of seconds.

"'Thank you! Oh, thank you, teacher!' she said, flexing her elbow.

"The stream of people continued for nearly an hour under torchlight. Several nearsighted or partially blind people came by and received perfect vision. Others on crutches hobbled up and walked, ran, or danced away. Many parents brought children to touch the teacher's sleeve. As they left, people thanked the teacher and praised God. A few could not leave, but instead slumped to the ground or pitched over backward when they received their healings. For these, the teacher's friends offered a lift and a gentle ride to the left of the large, flat rock where they maintained a space for these to recover their ability to walk.

"This group of overwhelmed healing recipients fascinated me. Many of them wept as if a close relative had died, others laughed hysterically, but most lay silent and peaceful.

"This brought to mind the traumas of my various surgical procedures over the years, and how long it takes after major surgery to regain one's bearings and to feel normal again. It made sense to me, in that context, that some who instantly received this miraculous healing also required time to adjust to their new conditions. But more to the point, I thought of the emotional impact of going from desperately sick to perfectly well in a matter of seconds. Who could ever hope for such a thing to happen to them, let alone have the capacity to contain it serenely when it did?

"The teacher's thinking also intrigued me, because his role seemed to have become, at least physically, passive. He leaned on his makeshift chair, seemingly content to watch as the people passed by and touched him. I'm quite sure that I've never in this life seen anyone so tired yet so content. His friends held a cup to his lips once in a while or placed a piece of fruit or bread into his mouth. He received this ministry placidly, with a grateful smile.

"A man whose right side seemed effectively paralyzed dragged himself to where the teacher sat. He touched the teacher's sleeve with his left hand, but nothing appeared to happen immediately. He remained before the teacher, as though waiting for something to occur. The teacher said, 'Go on; you are healed.' The man dragged his bad leg behind him one step, and then began to shake his right arm as if to wake it from sleep. With the next step he nearly stumbled, as his right leg straightened suddenly. With each pace, his step grew stronger and more even. He raised his right arm and rotated it, demonstrating its restoration. After that, he fairly skipped into the night.

"Two shy girls, about twelve years old, I'd say, approached the teacher next. One had a bandaged wrist; the other walked with a limp and used a walking stick. When they each touched the teacher, unrestrained giggling exploded from them. They showed each other their wonderfully well limbs and then collapsed in a heap of hysterical laughter. They landed far enough to one side so as not to block the line. Their laughter became background music for dozens of healings that followed.

"A large man waddled up to the teacher. He must have had bad hips because he walked as if his feet were attached to a bar. He probably would have been in a wheelchair were he alive today. There was no such option for him, of course, and it pained me to watch his slow progress. He brushed his work-hardened fingers across the teacher's sleeve. Two loud pops and his mouth sprang open. The big man whooped and the two girls on the ground in front of him laughed louder. He caught their contagious hilarity as he freely moved, like a man drunk with joy, into the darkness of the hillside.

"A lone boy, a mousy little slip of a youngster, sidled up. He barely brushed the teacher's sleeve then grabbed his throat. 'Hey!' he said. As he walked away, I could hear him hooting and hollering for quite a while as he moved through the crowd. Little waves of laughter followed his progress down the hill.

"In line after the boy, a man shuffled forward. I heard his labored breathing even in the crowded out of doors. In fact, he appeared to relax and his breathing seemed to improve just *before* he touched the sleeve of the teacher's robe. After a brief touch, he sucked in large breaths, his ribcage fully expanding as we walked away. He breathed out a few hearty Alleluias as he moved away.

"Close on his heals came an older woman whose hands shook uncontrollably. I surmised she had Parkinson's disease, or something similar to it. Ironically, the instant she touched the teacher's robe she began to shake more violently. She fell at the feet of Simon the Zealot, who broke her fall by catching her with one hand. Mary rushed over and helped Simon move the woman out of the pathway, but it took only a few more seconds before the violent healing tremors dissipated, revealing that the Parkinson's tremors were gone as well. The teacher's two friends helped her to her feet.

"'Thank you. Oh, bless you, teacher. Thank you so much,' she said, her words tripping over each other.

"Meanwhile, a couple with a baby cradled in what must have been the father's arms stepped tentatively toward the teacher. In the light of the torches behind the teacher, I saw that the baby was ashen in color.

"The teacher held up his hands to take the baby from them. The father handed the little one to the teacher. Peter and John looked at each other as if checking to see if the other would intervene or offer assistance, perhaps unsure that the exhausted teacher would be able to hold even this small child. Clearly the teacher found a reserve of energy with which to take the baby in his hands. Peering down into the baby's pale face, he instructed the mother, 'Put your hand on her chest.'

"The woman looked briefly at her husband and then complied. As soon as the mother touched her, the baby seemed to awaken. Her arms and legs pumped, she turned her head toward her parents. Both of them burst into tears of joy. The little one squirmed, reaching out for her mother.

"As the little family made their way back into the crowd, a stream of people moved steadily past the teacher. I don't know how many of these suffered from illnesses and deformities that were not comfortable topics for a public gathering, but it occurred to me that this latter means of healing was particularly advantageous, because the teacher didn't ask about their injuries or diseases and they didn't need to tell him.

"It had grown quite dark by this time, and the teacher finally allowed his friends to stop the flow of sick and suffering people. Peter announced that the rest of those waiting would have to let the teacher sleep until morning, when he would begin to heal again. This last phrase received a gigantic chorus of cheers that tapered into mixed sobs and laughter.

"I overheard several people repeating the word 'morning,' with breathy relief and tired smiles.

"'I was worried that this would be the only day,' I heard a woman say to the man with her.

"'Imagine having to walk home with this sore foot of mine,'

the man said in reply.

"The teacher took a deep breath, the sort one hears in bed next to you just before your spouse falls to sleep.

"His friends conferred briefly about where to go.

"Philip spoke. 'I have a spot over here.' He gestured toward the rocks behind them. 'Joanna and Matthew and some others are holding the place for us.'

"'I'm glad somebody thought ahead,' Peter said, patting Phillip on the back.

"James and Andrew helped the teacher to his feet, each holding an arm around his waist as he draped his tired arms over their shoulders. They very nearly carried him the fifty yards to the sheltered place among the rocks that Matthew, Judas, and Bartholomew guarded.

"The women, including Salome, Joanna, and Mary, arranged a fire, food, bedding, and a covering for the teacher and his friends. Someone had given them a large fish, caught in the lake at the bottom of the hill. James set to cleaning the fish with professional efficiency, while Salome nurtured a small flame.

"All around them, campfires flickered yellow in the night. Some of the fuel for those fires came from the accumulated pile of discarded crutches and stretchers. The atmosphere resembled a summer campground or a large community celebration. Laughter and singing rose from every direction. Many people still waited for their healing, but most of these had certainly seen enough that day to feel assured that tomorrow they too would be healed.

"None had been turned away, no disease proved too difficult, no person unworthy to approach the teacher, no oppression powerful enough to resist his assault. Everyone who made their way to the teacher had received healing, freedom, or even resurrection. In that place, with the teacher in their midst, no one need fear sickness, injury, spiritual oppression, emotional pain, or even death.

"His back against a large rock and cushioned by a blanket, the teacher sat near the newly lit fire, his feet stretched out toward it. He stared into the flames without moving. His friends had convinced him to sit up long enough for them to get him some substantial food; and he was a good patient for those many caregivers watching over him.

"His friends gathered around the fire, some bringing firewood, others carrying gifts of food from the people camping around them. Some swept the area of small stones and sticks and began laying out sleeping mats and blankets. Eventually, all of them surrounded the growing fire and helped with preparations for a well-earned meal.

"The talk mostly reflected on what had happened during that day. The teacher remained quiet but smiled at the humorous twists some of his friends put on what they had seen. He nodded as one and then another recalled a remarkable transformation. None of them had seen everything that happened, so they helped to complete the story of that day for one another.

"The teacher ate broiled fish, bread, and several small pieces of fruit. He drank both water and wine. Then he looked at Joanna with drooping eyes that clearly asked where she had planned for him to sleep. She smiled at the exhausted man and roused two of his friends to help him to a sleeping mat they had prepared for him.

"The evening was still warm enough that the fires were not needed for heat, though I expect the morning would dawn cool. Then, perhaps, the fires would have to be stirred to life against the chill of the arid hills as they rose for another day of miracles.

"The teacher lay by himself under a blanket, the hood of his cloak pulled up over his head. Once his eyes closed he appeared to fall asleep almost instantly. It seemed that he had spent all of the human energy he had. Now he slept peacefully to recharge his body.

"His friends talked, laughed, and teased one another, debated events and meanings, and eventually finished their meal. They began to disperse to their own sleeping arrangements as the fire glowed red and the insects and frogs took over the night air with their own conversations."

After Walter finished this last narration, Jillian wept openly.

And He Healed Them All

Actually, she sobbed, her thin frame surging and subsiding. I don't fully understand why I didn't join her. I certainly felt the finality of more than just the story of the dreams. I also had the feeling that the end of the dreams meant that Walter's life would end soon, as irrational as that sounds.

As I sat holding her hand, I wondered if Jillian's tide of tears vicariously released some of that mourning for Walter and me. I expect that a big part of our reserve was the fear of what would happen if we did let go and joined Jillian's emotional purge.

When Jillian's sobbing and gasping had slowed, I looked from her to Walter. "Thank you, Walter."

That's all I could manage. Jillian concurred with a brief renewal of her tears. Walter just pursed his lips in silence.

Chapter Fifteen
Waking Up after the Dreams

Though they didn't all come on consecutive days, but over the course of more than three weeks, Walter had recounted major parts of twelve dreams that we stitched together into one day in the life of Jesus. At the beginning I hesitated to absorb two important ideas.

First, Jesus did heal everyone in a large mixed crowd without exception or excuse. Second, Walter was seeing this historical event portrayed vividly, almost cinematically, in this series of dreams. Even without Walter's dreams, the notion that Jesus healed everyone who came to him was revolutionary to me, a bit of Scripture I had neglected since I'd first heard of it as a child. But Walter's dreams seemed designed to revive the memory of that Sunday school lesson and to bring it as a challenge to my adult self, a challenge that rocked me off my foundation.

Later that week, after the final dream, I visited Walter at the nursing home. It was one of those February days that hold the promise of spring. I had no afternoon classes and didn't resist the call to get outside and absorb some warm sunshine. At that time of year, sixty degrees seems balmy in these parts.

Walter was in the lounge playing Hearts with three of his friends. I sat and watched until they finished a hand before I persuaded him to come out with me for some fresh air. We walked across the street and then made a leisurely lap around the park. The trees had no leaves to shade us yet, but who wants shade on the warmest day of a northern February?

After that one lap, we sat on a park bench with our backs to the nursing home. The wind gently pushed a lock of his thin gray hair across Walter's forehead. He made a habitual and ineffective brush at it.

"How are classes?"

My bout of spring fever induced by the weather clouded the answer to that question. More than that, however, the pressure I felt to account for the truth of those dreams in the way I taught remained a deeply irritating piece of unfinished business.

"It gets to be a habit after a while. I can easily go through the motions, recycling the syllabus from last year, and saying the same old things."

Walter turned his head toward me. "Is that what you're doing?"

I nodded. "It's the default I slip into while I try to tame the wild animals warring inside my head."

He raised his eyebrows and sat up a bit straighter. "That sounds pretty serious."

I laughed a short and cheerless laugh. "Oh, I don't mean you should call the exorcist or anything like that. But I know what I heard from your dreams demands a difference in me that I'm not seeing yet. Teaching those young people in that traditionally Protestant college would seem like an obvious place to start."

"So what's holding you back?"

I tipped my head toward Walter. "You're not gonna let me off easy on this, are you?"

He squinted against the bright sunlight, so that it was hard to tell how much of a smile he was wearing. "Of course, I took this journey with you," he said. "I know the impact it would have on any perceptive and sensitive person. And I know the images of Jesus pouring himself out and setting all those people free opened my eyes more than any spiritual experience in all my life." He took a deep breath, as if talking for so long was a strain. "For me it's much easier to respond to that than it is for you, I know. I got to live in those dreams."

I wanted to back away one step from where I knew this was headed. "I'm still working on what I believe. I'm not to the part where I allow this revelation to overhaul my life."

He uncrossed and recrossed his feet at the ankles. For a moment, it seemed to me that he was unusually fascinated by being able to do that, carefully observing how it worked so well, but I dodged that distraction.

I tried to dig deeper. "One thing I've had to face," I said, "is the realization that deep down I assume God can't really heal everything, that some things are too hard even for God. But the stories of Jesus healing everyone in the crowd don't support my gut assumption. It's as if I think of myself as so exceptional that I would be the one person in the crowd that he can't heal."

Walter picked up my point and drove it home. "And the sticky part of that trap is that it seems like it's humility to think that I might be the one exception, when really it's a sort of pride."

I seldom came to Walter for back-patting comfort. More often he made me more uncomfortable with insights like that. He remained my teacher until the end.

Even in the throes of this profound conversation, I could see Walter struggling to keep his eyes open, reminding me of an old cat sitting in a tract of sunshine on a familiar rug.

"There's time for a nap before dinner," I said.

He looked at me, slightly startled, and the airy and unfocused way he responded made him seem old all over again. "Huh? Oh, yes. I guess I could use some rest."

"C'mon, I'll help you up." I stood and offered a hand as he gathered his strength to return to his feet and wander back to his room.

Walter sat on his bed and made no complaint when I helped him slip off his shoes.

"Thanks, James," he said, mumbling slightly.

"Have a good rest, Walter."

He placed his glasses on his nightstand and lay back on his pillow.

I closed the door behind me, stopping at the nurse's station to let them know not to disturb his nap.

The next evening, a Friday, I went to dinner with Jillian at her favorite Mexican restaurant, one that I hadn't explored before. The warm aromas of cumin, corn tortillas and roasted chilies stirred my growing appetite.

"Chicken enchiladas molè is my favorite here," she said as we opened our menus.

I peeked across the top of the heavy, plastic-coated menu and caught Jillian peeking back at me.

"What are you looking at?" She played the part of the shy girl pretty well.

"I was just enjoying how you're content to simply tell me what's your favorite, without trying to get me to like the same thing."

"It sounds like you have some history with that kind of game."

I laughed, shrugging slightly. "Don't know where you would get that idea."

"Mmmm," was all she said.

"I'm not really hard to persuade," I said. "But I'm really only an easy sale for people like Walter, and you, who know that pushing only gets push back."

"So I have you under my spell, do I?"

"It's not obvious?"

She smiled and returned to the menu.

"You know, if this relationship keeps going on like this, someday we're gonna have to describe how we met," I said

Now she laughed out loud, straightening up only a little to say, "Well, that's why you have to write the book, so it's easier for people to believe."

"Hmmm." It was my turn for an inarticulate response. "You think people will believe the story about the dreams? I believe it only because I know and trust Walter. Without that the whole thing seems incredible."

"That's not surprising. Most people only hold their most important beliefs because of someone they know and trust believing right along with them, or perhaps before them. Maybe you're just supposed to be the first one Walter convinces."

As with Walter, earlier in the week, I felt like Jillian was assuming that my faith level was well above where I would have placed it. Or was it just that I didn't know faith even when I had it? Maybe they were right and I was just being too hard on myself.

"Well, I know Walter wants me to write it up, and I would welcome some way to honor him, so I think I will give it a try."

"And maybe in the process you'll get more clarity on just what's real and what you can believe in."

The waitress arrived to take our orders, giving me a break to consider Jillian's speculation. The conversation faded in other directions as we ate chips and salsa followed by entrées, which we each enjoyed intensely. When I finally decided I had eaten all I could without regretting it, I thought again of having to tell someone how Jillian and I met.

"Did Walter ever tell you how he met Carolyn, his wife?"

Jillian wiped her lips with a cloth napkin and shook her head. "No, he hasn't said much to me about his wife."

I took a sip of water and tried to sort out the story. "If I remember right, Walter was studying in England, at Cambridge University. He was in his early twenties, something of a prodigy, and got some kind of scholarship a few years after the war." I sat back, trying to get more comfortable after so much rich and spicy food.

"Carolyn was traveling through Europe with some girlfriends, privileged girls with money and time, and a desire to see the world. I always thought of Carolyn as something of a tomboy when she was young, for her sense of adventure, her love for the outdoors, and her tendency to wear men's jackets or shirts. She was an artist, a painter, and that was part of her style."

"Anyway, these young women had toured the old university and Carolyn was on her own one afternoon, sketching some ancient building or other. She sees this young scholar in a tweed jacket, sucking on a tobacco pipe, though nothing burning in it, and thinks he's a local she can ask about the history of the building she's sketching. The way Walter tells it, he put on his best British accent and made up some nonsense about the building to cover his complete ignorance of the architecture and history."

I remembered Walter and Carolyn's comic banter over the details of this encounter. "Carolyn claimed that she suspected something wasn't quite right with this pretender, though I think she couldn't put her finger on it. What they agreed about when they told me the story is that she didn't say anything to challenge Walter's pretense but went back to her sketching when he marched off triumphantly, under the impression he had completely fooled the American girl. But, as he was walking away, Walter realized he was attracted to the beautiful artist and wanted to get to know her. He knew he'd have to fess up about his real citizenship, with his real Midwestern accent, so he stuffed his pipe into his pocket and went back, hat in hand, to apologize for the masquerade and find out her name." I laughed more at the memory of the disputed versions of the story between Walter and Carolyn than the story itself.

Jillian joined my laughter, watching me with appreciatively sparkling eyes. But my mind turned back to Walter as my mentor and friend, twenty-some years ago, when I first heard that story in his back garden, him still a professor with a respected following in school and even a national reputation in his field. And I recalled Carolyn serving us tea, which had prompted the England memories. I could picture her wearing one of Walter's old fedoras that day, to keep the sun out of her eyes as she sketched a lilac bush next to the patio.

Carolyn had been gone now several years, and Walter seemed destined to follow her soon. Jillian's gaze awaited me when I forced myself to reverse away from that anxious thought.

"I think I'll go see Walter again tomorrow," I said, to myself as much as to Jillian.

In fact, I visited Walter three more times at the home. Each time he seemed a bit more tired. I particularly remember the last time we visited.

I found him sitting in the comfy chair in his room, a book on his lap, his head back, and eyes closed. I assumed he was asleep and hesitated about whether to come in and wait for him to wake up or to visit again another day. But my momentary halt made enough of a disturbance to alert Walter. He opened his eyes without moving his head and looked at me.

"James." His voice crackled like a distant AM radio station.

"How are you, Walter?" I said, just as I had done dozens of times before.

"Tired but happy." He raised his head and looked more squarely at me. He picked up the worn hardcover book and put his bookmark in place. He closed it and perched it on his lap.

"Seems like you've been more tired lately. You keeping late hours with one of your lady friends?"

Walter grinned his sly fox grin and wheezed a laugh, as if his soul was amused but his body refused to commit to fully expressing it.

"Is that laugh a confession of guilt?"

He shook his head. "I'm denying everything." He grabbed a couple of gulps of air. His breathing seemed almost conscious instead of instinctual natural breathing. He saw my furrowed brow after those obvious gasps for air.

"Oh, don't look so worried. I'm feeling no pain, and that's without meds."

I acknowledged his encouragement but made no promise not to worry. I perched on the edge of his bed, but he moved to hand me the book in his lap. I rose to take it and lay it on his nightstand. Collapsed again into his sedate pose, his weary smile reminded me of his description of Jesus healing people at the end of the day, both more tired and more peaceful than anyone he had ever seen. Perhaps Walter had received some of that same grace to be both weak and content at the same time.

"You see Jillian last night?"

"Yep."

"Good. You hang on to that one."

That was the first time Walter had given me any kind of relationship advice since my divorce, and he offered it without caveat or moderation.

"You really like her, huh?"

He nodded. "So do you."

I laughed. "You've taken up mind reading in your old age?"

"Doesn't take a mind reader," he said, his voice faint and yet confident.

We didn't say much more, but before I left that last time, he stopped me and strung together more words than I thought he could manage at the time.

"You know, James, I'm very happy that I got to share these past several weeks with you. It meant so much more to have you along for the ride."

That was the last thing Walter said to me. That night, less than two weeks after he received the last of the life-changing dreams, Walter Schrader died in his sleep.

I knew what had happened as soon as I got the call from the morning nurse. I knew he had flown away to hover over those dusty hills again, to see a glimpse of heaven on earth, before making the flight to that much better resting place.

That Jillian was there to help me arrange for Walter's cremation and memorial service, including contacting his relatives, made the experience more tolerable. Walter had no children. I had become his *de facto* son and the executor of his estate. However, I still managed to feel like an outsider among his friends and family at the memorial service. There, too, Jillian's presence comforted me greatly.

After the service and the reception, the crowd of unfamiliar people and the crush of disorienting emotions, Jillian and I walked to my car. We stood in the parking lot outside the Presbyterian church where Walter had been an elder and long-time member. She stopped and faced me when we reached her side of the car. Our eyes locked.

She wrapped her arms around my waist, and I drew her close to me. I allowed the energy of my pain and loss to fill that embrace. Jillian stayed with me, holding tight.

"You know, I've been thinking about why God healed Walter

from his stroke, only to have him die soon after," I said, loosening my grip.

Jillian leaned back and squinted, as if she was sizing me up.

"It reminds me of a time when I was a small boy and my father was on a business trip to Detroit," I said. "The night he was due to drive home, there was a terrible snowstorm. I remember my mother checking the clock repeatedly, and looking outside every time a car drove past. When she said good night to me, I guess she could see in my quiet seriousness that I had inherited some of her anxiety. She tried to assure me, but I still had a hard time falling asleep. Much later that night, my father woke me up out of a fitful sleep to let me know that he had gotten home safely. After that, I slept more peacefully."

Jillian's face lighted at the analogy, but she waited for me to state my punch line.

"So, I see Walter getting healed before he died as like my dad waking me up so I could sleep more peacefully."

Jillian's smile broadened.

I released my embrace and took her hands. "Walter changed my life more than once," I said.

She searched my eyes as if for the signs that would help her follow where I was going. Then she grinned and tilted her head slightly. "Mine too."

Chapter Sixteen
The Teacher Who Changed My Life

Over my decades of teaching ethics in that college, with its religious foundations and modern intellectual reputation, I had refined a pair of approaches to enlightening young minds about how to live an ethically defensible life. The first tact led us through the lineage of philosophers who had survived the winnowing process of historians and subsequent philosophers, examining what they taught about the nature of right and wrong. On this trail I would carefully and respectfully set up each of these intellectual predecessors, displaying their system of belief as well as I could. Then I would tear it down, revealing its inherent weakness, often with the help of the next philosophical titan listed on the syllabus. And so it would go until all of the great minds had been vanquished, leaving us with a smug satisfaction that they were no greater than we are and at the same time offering little hope of truth or direction in life.

The second approach focused on the great hot-button issues of our day: sex, wealth, power, the sanctity of life, etc. While picking through the particulars of each of these contemporary questions, often in light of previous historical debates, we would examine the various options. Regarding protecting the environment, for example, we studied laissez-faire capitalism, which expected market forces to keep us from totally destroying the planet on which we all depend for life, and we studied extreme environmentalism, which verges on worshipping the planet and regales modern humans with a long list of accusations regarding our ill-treatment of Mother Earth. Where we end up then is some version of collapsing the defenses of the extremes by showing that they stand upon presuppositions that most of us didn't share, and opting for a more balanced approach. Of course, as the professor, I got first crack at defining *balanced*.

Through the years, I had attempted to offer some options for building a system on which to base a virtuous life, as Aristotle called it. I showed my students that the various, and often sharply opposed, viewpoints we studied in class all boiled down to two questions: What do you value? And how do you sort between your own *competing* values? In answering those questions I had relied much more on the intellectual heritage of the college than I did on religious or biblical foundations. This left me with more of a philosophical framework than a compelling passion, and changed no one's life, including my own.

On a Tuesday in March, not long after Walter's death, a young man met me after class and asked me a simple question. We had been discussing various approaches to violence and war in class that day, and, as usual, I had danced in and out of several answers, with the intention of encouraging those young minds to examine the options and form their own beliefs.

Randy Hamer, a pale nineteen-year-old with hair cut close on one side and hanging to his collar on the other, looked at me with his one visible eye and asked, "What do you believe?"

I gathered up my folder of class materials and my tablet computer and prepared for my usual evasive maneuvers to avoid directly answering that common inquiry. My justification for this practice was that I didn't want these young, impressionable students to adopt my beliefs just because I could make a good argument. It was better for them to form their own beliefs, so they had something to take with them when they had forgotten what we discussed in class and even the professor's name.

As Randy followed me from the classroom to my office, where I had office hours to keep, I found myself faltering in my usual "what really matters is what you believe" speech. Something was interfering with that ready response, something perhaps about the way that thin and intense young man attended to my words, even as we wound our way through streams of students and faculty flowing to and from classes.

"But what about your personal beliefs?" Randy persisted, as we reached the third floor of the creaky old building that housed the philosophy department. One of my colleagues passed us in the thin corridor outside my office trying to pretend he wasn't listening to my response. I caught his eye and he picked up his pace, surrendering his attempt to capture some sort of personal commitment to truth from one who had long avoided getting pinned down.

I stepped through my office door and stopped myself from reasserting that Randy had to form his own beliefs. A look into that one big brown eye in his expectant, face and the intensity of his persistent questioning hinted that this young man was looking for real answers, not just an opening in my system that he could use to argue against me. Walter and his dreams climbed out of my memory and into my cluttered office.

I motioned for Randy to have a seat in one of the little circle of chairs in the corner, not content to speak to him across my broad, paper-laden desk. He slouched into an armchair and dropped his backpack to the side, pushing his hair out of the way and revealing that he really did have two eyes. I dropped my folder and tablet on the corner of my desk and resisted checking email before sitting down in a chair facing Randy.

I asked him a question to see where he was starting from. "What's your church background, Randy?"

That seemed to wake him up, like a poke in the ribs. He raised his thin, dark eyebrows. "Well, my parents made me go to the Methodist church all my life, but they never said I had to believe any of what I was taught there. It was pretty hard to figure out what they believed there anyway, one Sunday school teacher saying one thing about God and the preacher saying something else. The people who made the most sense to me, even if I disagreed with most of what they said, was the Young Life group at school. I liked the kids there so I hung out with them and listened without arguing."

I couldn't tell if Randy was customizing this answer to appeal to me, or to project a more intellectual image of himself. But I decided to tell him about some changes in my faith, inspired by Walter's dreams.

After I finished describing who Walter was, and then doing my best to concisely portray the extraordinary dreams, I could see Randy fading backward under the weight of incredulity. Having already decided to take this risky direction, I pushed further and asked what he was thinking.

He shook his head so that his long bangs fell down over his eye again. "I can't believe it."

"Which part don't you believe?" I hoped for some divine inspiration to help me communicate the reality and power of Walter's experience.

"No, it's not that I don't believe what you're saying." He appeared to waver for a moment. "What I'm having a hard time believing is that I had this dream a couple of days ago, that an old professor I didn't know was going to show me these pictures of something he'd discovered. And when I showed up at his office, in some building I've never been in, he told me he couldn't show me because the things he had discovered were hidden in his dreams."

Stunned, I checked that my mouth wasn't hanging open.

"Wow," was all I could say. My lips and tongue had suddenly gone dusty dry.

I looked hard at Randy, checking to see a twitch or twinge revealing a joke, uncovering a deception. But he looked concerned, like he was afraid I was going to keel over or something.

I laughed, all of this stunned disbelief feeling strangely familiar to me.

"Why does everyone around me get these dreams, but not me?" I said, without filtering the accuracy of what just leaked out me.

He shrugged. "What do you think it means?"

"Of course, it means that there's something in Walter's dreams that you need to see. But you're asking something more than that, right?"

"Yeah, like, why me? Why now? What did I do? Or what am I supposed to do?"

I offered half a grin and cocked an eyebrow. "What are you supposed to do?" Though I had a cascade of questions, I had one answer for Randy. "I think you should listen to Walter tell about his dreams. I have most of his narration in MP3 files." I waited for Randy to reject my prescription, but he sat as if waiting for more.

"I'd love to listen to them again," I said. "Maybe we could listen together and talk about what's in there."

If you ever saw the look on a kid's face when he asks for less than what he really wants and you offer all of what he was secretly hoping for, you can imagine the birthday morning kind of smile that flashed across Randy's face . . . before he ducked back behind his cool college intellectual facade.

He nodded. "Yeah, I think that would be good."

I called Jillian at work to see if she had time for me to tell her about Randy. She was leaving her office, headed to her mom's place, and then home. She suggested I meet her at her place to eat leftovers and tell her what happened. That sounded even better than my plan.

***

"I hate throwing away food," Jillian said as she pulled a plastic container out of the microwave, shifting it quickly between hands and dropping it onto the counter. I carefully pried the lid to let the steam out without getting scalded.

"I know what you mean." I let the condensation drip into the sink as I pulled the lid off all the way. "It comes from being raised by people who were kids during World War II."

Jillian laughed. "My mom would be very quick to point out how that was impossible. She's much too young for that to be the case." She mimicked the protesting tone I imagined her mother would have used.

Filling our plates and moving to her kitchen table, we settled down to eat. But first Jillian pointed out something.

"You see how comfortable I am with you now? Eating leftovers at the kitchen table? Clearly I'm past trying to impress you."

I patted her hand. "You never had to try."

She grinned, rolled her eyes slightly, and actually blushed, resorting to eating instead of responding to my flirtation.

After a hot bite and a quick drink of water, she changed the subject. "So what did you want to tell me?"

Her question renewed my excitement over what happened with Randy and I replayed my meeting with him, forgetting about my food until it was plenty cool enough to eat.

"The plan is to get together once a week or so and listen to Walter's recordings. I figure I can make some notes and even get some help from Randy for writing up the story in the dreams. He's a good writer, one of those students whose work is a joy to read."

Jillian sat with her hand over her mouth, shaking her head persistently. I felt like I had wowed her, but then knew I didn't deserve any of the credit. All I did was take one small risk at mentioning Walter's dreams to a student. I didn't do anything to orchestrate the dreams of two people who would never meet each other.

"Remember how Walter said he thought the dreams were for you and me, but also for other people?" Jillian said, a honey-smooth hush tempering her voice.

I got another one of those chills up my back and wondered if maybe I should start getting used to that. I huffed a small laugh then leveled off. My attention turned to wishing Walter was there to hear about how his dreams would live on after him.

"So what do you think is in the dreams that Randy's supposed to see?" Jillian had set her fork down and apparently forgotten her food.

"The same things that Walter saw, and you and I saw. That God loved people so much that, through his son, he had compassion on a whole motley crowd, received all who came to him and healed them all."

Then I realized something. "You know, I think, if Walter and God have their way, I'm gonna start believing it's true."

Acknowledgments:

With so many rewrites over a long period, there are a lot of people to thank. First of all there's my Dad who encouraged me with his enthusiasm for the early drafts. The original inspiration for the earliest drafts came from Mark Cornthwaite—someone I've lost track of by now. My biggest fans for the first edition of the published book were my sisters, whose encouragement helped keep me motivated to improve this story.

My lovely wife has paid the highest price for all the time and energy I've put into this, not to mention reading and proof reading early drafts, for which I'm extremely grateful.

Finally, I must thank Erin Brown, an able and accomplished editor, who showed me how to transform this book into what it is today. She deserves lots of credit for pointing me in the right direction on several issues. I recommend her services highly.

Printed in Great Britain
by Amazon